THE OLD WOMA

THE OLD WOMAN AND THE RIVER

A NOVEL BY ISMAIL FAHD ISMAIL

TRANSLATED BY SOPHIA VASALOU

Interlink Books

An imprint of Interlink Publishing Group, Inc.
Northampton, Massachusetts

First published in 2019 by

Interlink Books
An imprint of Interlink Publishing Group, Inc.
46 Crosby Street, Northampton, MA 01060
www.interlinkbooks.com

  Published as part of the Swallow Editions series.
Founder and Series Editor: Rafik Schami

Library of Congress Cataloging-in-Publication Data
Names: Ismāʿīl, Ismāʿīl Fahd, author. | Vasalou, Sophia, translator.
Title: The old woman and the river : a novel / by Ismail Fahd Ismail; translated by
    Sophia Vasalou.
Other titles: Subaylīyāt. English
Description: Northampton, MA : Interlink Books, 2019. | Summary: "After the
    ceasefire in 1988, the devastation to the landscape of Iraq wrought by the longest
    war of the twentieth century—the Iran-Iraq War—becomes visible. Yet, surveying
    this destruction from the sky, a strip of land bursting with green can be seen. The
    secret of this fertility, sustaining villages and remaining soldiers, is unclear. But it
    is said that one old woman is responsible for this lifeline"-- Provided by publisher.
Identifiers: LCCN 2019027948 | ISBN 9781623719821 (paperback)
Subjects: LCSH: Civilians in war--Iraq--Fiction. | Iran-Iraq War, 1980-1988—
    Environmental aspects--Fiction.
Classification: LCC PJ7838.S556 S8213 2019 | DDC 892.7/36--dc23
LC record available at https://lccn.loc.gov/2019027948

Printed and bound in the United States of America

AUTHOR'S FOREWORD

ONE DAY IN LATE AUTUMN of 1988, I got a call from a journalist friend working at the Kuwaiti newspaper *Public Opinion*. "One of the last times we met, you mentioned you come from a village south of Basra—"

"Sabiliyat," I volunteered.

"Now listen to this," he replied.

The story went as follows. A few weeks after the Iran-Iraq war wound to a close, the Iraqi authorities invited the press to take stock of the devastation the war had caused. His newspaper handed that assignment to him. They gathered the journalists—foreign and Arab—inside the only serving lounge of Basra-Ma'qil airport. There they split them into groups in three helicopters and flew them over the coastal strip to the west of Shatt al-Arab and down toward the Port of Al-Faw.

The reporters were stunned to see the groves of date palm trees. All withered, their leaves had everywhere turned a bright yellow. That's war for you—eight long years had turned nature upside down. But then all of a sudden the yellow vanished. They found themselves flying over a strip of land bursting with green. It was like a lush oasis of some kind, no more than a couple of kilometers wide, beginning from the Shatt al-Arab and coming to a halt at the fringes of the western desert. After that, the yellow reasserted itself. Pointing to the green strip, my friend asked: "Why just *this* bit of land—?" The answers he received failed to satisfy him. All he got out of one of the conductors was, "That's the village of Sabiliyat."

Having finished his account, my journalist friend said to me, "Since you come from there, you should be the one to uncover the secret."

As the war between Iraq and Iran began to gather steam in the second half of 1980, the Iraqi authorities issued a directive.

"Out of regard for the safety of citizens residing in villages and towns adjacent to the areas of hostilities, we decree as follows..." Um Qasem recalls a military jeep fitted with a loud-speaker driving down the main road of the village. The voice was stern. "All inhabitants are requested to vacate their homes within seventy-two hours." Whenever people asked where to, they were met with the answer, "Other provinces in the country have been given resources to accommodate evacuees coming from the Basra area." This was always accompanied by a reassurance. "The present state of mobilization will not last more than three months. After that, everything will return to normal."

Um Qasem racks her brain to remember more. She sees the first day drifting by in a daze. "How can we go, leaving all our ties to this place behind?" As well, an important question weighs on her mind, just as much as it does on the minds of her husband, her three sons, and two daughters—"What will happen to our nine donkeys?"

That night no one in the family could find a moment's sleep. The next morning they were surprised to discover how the other villagers were reacting. Most of them had already started packing their bags. Everyone had acquaintances or relatives living somewhere or other in the country. Um Qasem's family gathered together to confer. "What are we to do?"

"Our surviving relatives are in Al-Ahsa," her husband said. "One thing that's certain is that getting there requires crossing international borders, which means traveling papers for everyone. With all the fighting, there's not much hope on that score. Our only option is to head north until we find land big enough for us and the donkeys."

Her reply to her husband's words drifts back to her. "I don't think we'll find a piece of land that suits us." She recalls his acknowledgment, and the pained sigh that preceded it. "God's land is big enough for everyone."

The decision to depart for an indefinite destination took up the whole of the next day. The effort to determine which of their belongings to pack onto the donkeys and which to abandon to an unknown fate took up the whole of the third day. A little before sunset, they were surprised to see another military vehicle driving up and down the street announcing, "Anyone found in breach of the evacuation order will be subject to imprisonment and fines." But Um Qasem says that her family were not the kind of people to disobey orders. They deliberated about which goods to take with them, picking out clothes, furnishings, cooking utensils, identity documents, and at dawn they set off with their packed-up donkeys, heading north.

Moving along, the first hour after their departure, Um Qasem remembers her eldest son Qasem's remark as they were crossing the bridge at Hebaba River, approaching the dirt track that led to Sanqar village.

"If we hadn't had the donkeys with us, we could have taken a taxi and everything would have been quicker."

She recalls the reply her middle son Hameed had shot back.

"We'd never find a taxi willing to take us."

"Why not?"

"Because we're a mob of twenty-odd people."

At the time, Um Qasem recoiled, amazed at her sons' ability to make light banter when faced with a sudden turn of fortune that harbored unknown evil. She hears her husband's reprimand, "There is no strength but in God," and her heart leaps in her chest despite herself.

Her husband suffered from a serious illness that doctors called "cardiac insufficiency." They had warned him years ago.

"The choice is yours—either you give up smoking or make up your mind that death will come as a bolt from the blue."

He chose the first option, but a serious illness of this type requires ongoing treatment, which comes at a price. Three months before that, he had stopped buying the medication.

"It's no use."

Hearing him say these words was like watching him throw away the means to go on living.

Once she had asked him what the pain was like, and he had flashed her a bitter smile.

"Like being crushed between two massive rocks."

Even though she hadn't quite understood, she'd nodded in comprehension and listened attentively.

"Pain is one of the faces of death. When it takes hold of a person, he prays to his Lord to reclaim what's His, hoping to be relieved from suffering."

"You think nothing of leaving me on my own?" she had reproached him.

"You have children and grandchildren to take my place," was his answer.

It grated on her soul that he had died on the third night of their journey north. It angered her just as much as it pained her that he had been affectionate with her that night, laughing with pleasure and embracing life with all its limitations. He had gone to sleep, and when he was late getting out of bed at sunrise she chided him for his laziness, and he was unresponsive.

In order to be able to identify his grave, they buried him between two wild date palms growing right next to each other by the international highway on the northern outskirts of the city of Nasiriya.

"In times of trouble, things usually forbidden are permitted," her eldest son Qasem said to her. "Given our circumstances, you aren't obliged to observe the period of ritual seclusion," he added.

That question had never crossed her mind, but the pain was too heavy to bear. She reproached her husband for leaving her without a word of goodbye. Her eyes and heart followed her sons and daughters, her sons' wives and her daughters' husbands, her grandsons and granddaughters, and all she saw was a flash of sorrow and a transient sense of loss. The living have a right to go on living, and the dead must go to the mercy of their Lord. But things were different for Um Qasem. For her it was about losing something intimate. When you lose a person you felt at home with and there's no way of making up for it, your pain thickens before you know it. It becomes a heavy lump sitting at the bottom of your throat. The man she belonged with was no longer by her side.

A few days into their journey, the men reached a consensus. They would put up on the southern side of the main graveyard at Najaf, the news being that some of those who had traveled from Basra had settled in that area. "As this is temporary, there's no harm setting up a few shacks any which way, just to put a roof over everyone's head," one of the men said.

They provided her a relatively spacious shack all to herself. She didn't say to them that Bu Qasem wasn't there and this was no time for luxuries. While he was alive, she took pains for his comfort. One time when he visited her dreams, he asked her plaintively, "When will we be reunited?"

Three weeks after their arrival, someone turned up asking to hire their donkeys to haul some bricks from a kiln near their living quarters to a construction site a few kilometers away. "It's through work that God sustains his creatures." The sons and the daughters' husbands sprang into action. "We won't quarrel about the price." Requests to hire their donkeys began to pour in. With their financial circumstances improving, her sons began to settle into the place. The three months specified in the evacuation order that had been issued to the villages and cities south of Basra came and went, and still no word on when it would be time to return.

The war in full swing, six months roll by. Children and grandchildren busily get on with their lives. Um Qasem's sense of time begins to follow a different rhythm, unrelated to the presence of her sons and grandchildren all around her. Time almost grinds to a halt. And this constant feeling presses down on her ribs, the feeling she's gasping for air every breath she takes. Longing for the place she was before, her mind perpetually crowded with memories, all of them connected to *there*—her childhood, being a young girl, Bu Qasem coming to ask for her hand...

One afternoon, her son Hameed had brought her an orange from the Najaf souk. Her heart skipped a beat. She remembered a time long before any of her sons had been born, she had come down with something, and she was astonished to see her husband entering the house with four oranges in his hands.

"Where did you get these?"

"From the Pasha's orchard," he replied.

She gave him an anxious look.

"Nothing dishonest," he reassured her. "They're a gift from Makki, the gardener at the Pasha's orchard."

It was the first time in her life she'd eaten an orange. Its taste was bewitching, unlike any other orange she ever tasted after that. She remembers the orchard. It faced the spot on the river where some of the village women would get together to wash their cooking utensils or clothes. They were separated from the orchard by Chouma River, which led out from the Shatt al-Arab.

Oh, my foolish heart, why this scattering? Her imagination rises into the air to take form there. The place where she'd lived is the taste and savor in her mouth, the image in her mind's eye. She feels herself drifting away. If only she could go back there. She shuts her eyes and sees her husband moving back and forth between their conjugal room and the Hilawi date tree, before heading for the donkeys' pen. She hears his voice inviting her, "Come here, my love." Whenever they were alone, he always insisted on calling her "my love." She opens her eyes.

12

Back in the present, everyone is busy with their lives. When they were still living in Sabiliyat, she used to look forward to the Day of Ashura so she could travel to Najaf and visit the holy shrines. But it's one thing to specially put aside a few days for a visit, and another to find yourself forced to live indefinitely in the precincts of these shrines, leaving behind the place where you used to be.

With the beginning of the following school year, the adults took steps to enroll the children in the schools of Najaf. Once they had disappeared into their schools, Um Qasem's loneliness set in more deeply. Two years had gone by since their departure. She gathered her sons and daughters around her and spoke to them openly.

"I can't stay here."

"What do you mean?"

"I feel like I'm suffocating."

"If you want, we can take you to a doctor who'll get to the bottom of your fatigue."

She didn't say to them, *It's not that kind of illness.* Those listening to her were incapable of grasping what was turning over in her spirit.

"I'll wait a couple more days and then decide."

Two days later they asked her, "Shall we take you to a doctor?"

No need to be concerned, she'd said. She felt better already. She knew them well. None of them took the homesickness she was suffering from seriously. She had made up her mind to make the long jouney home independently. They had their lives to live, and she had to look after hers.

Covering the distance from Najaf to Sabiliyat would be

no small feat. She had to think long and hard about the means, as well as about the preparations required, while keeping everything under wraps for fear that her grandchildren and children would gang up on her to stop her. *"We won't let you go through with this crazy stunt,"* they'd say. She conceded it *was* a crazy, foolhardy thing to do, and they could say her mind had grown feeble with age, if they wanted to. But at heart she was unable to reconcile herself with the prospect of remaining where she was for an indefinite duration with no end in sight. The thought of spending the remaining years of her life in Sabiliyat had taken hold of her and wouldn't let go.

She weighed the options. Many of her personal belongings she could do without, she had plenty of things back home. Still, the hardship of the journey remained. The idea of taking a taxi didn't cross her mind—civilian vehicles weren't allowed to enter areas evacuated on military grounds. She'd have to return home the same way she left, taking one of the donkeys and trusting it to lead the way. Donkeys have the sense to retrace their route back to where they came from.

She fell to thinking. She knew each and every one of her donkeys like the back of her hand. She knew their temperaments, their stamina, and also the way some of them could be surly and stubborn. Reflection led her to settle on a donkey that her husband had named "Good Omen" the day it was born.

There was one time when opportunities for work had dried up for several weeks on end. Worry had begun to eat away at her husband.

"If things continue this way, we'll be forced to borrow," he'd said.

The day their donkey gave birth, someone came knocking at the door in the morning. Any chance he could hire their donkey? Her husband's lips parted in a joyous grin.

"This little donkey is good luck." The decision came to him. "We'll call him 'Good Omen.'" That was five years ago. Their little donkey was now fully grown.

"Oh, Good Omen." Seizing the opportunity when the donkeys were all alone in the pen, Um Qasem began her whispering conversation with him. "You have the mettle to endure the hardships of the road, you have the perseverance, but you can also be peevish at times." She gazed deep into his eyes and continued in the same whisper. "Do you promise to look after me until we make it home to Sabiliyat?" Her words sank into Good Omen. He wasn't used to being addressed by any member of the family other than his old master, and he had disappeared. His senses went on high alert. What was Um Qasem proposing? Whatever she might have in mind, he was at her disposal. He flicked away a couple of flies with his tail and held out his head to her. She reached out and kneaded his neck with her hand. "I'll take you with me on condition that you don't bray."

The decision made, she began to make preparations. Um Qasem couldn't say for sure what the attitude of the army would be if they met her along the way or as she approached her destination. She knew she would do her utmost to convince them to allow her to return. Everyone dies when their time comes, be it in the midst of war or lying in their own bed. The effort to get ready for what the future might have in store had energized her. Getting hold of a bit of money for contingencies, thinking about a few provisions for the road, some dry dates and tahini pastries with oil and sugar, a can of drinking water. She didn't neglect to pack a sickle in case it came in handy. It would take her a week to reach Sabiliyat, maybe longer. She began paying daily visits to the donkeys' pen to make sure Good Omen understood what they were in for.

February came and went, only three weeks left till the Nowruz festival. Her hope was that when that day arrived, it would find her there. She decided that Friday would be the day of her departure. Everyone in her extended family took advantage of Fridays to sleep in, so she'd have a head start before they noticed she was missing.

Getting things ready, then setting out. She was gratified by the solidarity the donkeys showed her. They didn't start braying when she entered their pen at two in the morning, making do with only a few muffled snorts. She strapped her few supplies onto Good Omen's back, pulled her cloak tight around herself, and cast a final glance at the other donkeys. "I'll be seeing you," she whispered.

She thought it best not to mount Good Omen at the start. "I think you know the way," she said to him. She let him walk along in front of her. In a few minutes they had left behind the alleys that ran through the shanties of the evacuees, and they confronted an empty land that stretched out as far as the eye could see. Um Qasem noticed the palm tree groves standing a few minutes' walk to her left. If she happened to need drinking water, she could head over to them. All of a sudden she realized that Good Omen had come to a halt and was nodding toward her with his head. "I can still walk," she said to him. "The moment I feel tired I'll get on your back," she added. He refused to budge. She drew up to him and ran her hand over his neck.

"If you insist." She climbed onto his back and he instantly broke into a brisk trot. Had Um Qasem thought it over, she would have realized that with her small frame she was hardly a burden for Good Omen, compared with the stack of bricks weighing almost a quarter of a ton that crushed him as he wobbled his way from the kiln to the construction site several miles away through the crowded streets of Najaf.

After her husband died, she hadn't felt like touching food for days on end, provoking her children's and grandchildren's anxiety and pleas.

"If you go on with this hunger strike—"

"It's not a hunger strike."

They begged, they scolded her. "You look like someone who's decided to starve to death."

She relented and went back to taking her meals as usual. She knew how much they worried about her health. She remembers what Bu Qasem used to say to her.

"You have the figure of a gazelle."

She used to laugh. "A bag of bones."

The day of Nowruz. She remembers what her mother used to tell her. "I gave birth to you on the morning of Nowruz."

Some people like to celebrate when their birthday comes around. For her part, the only thing that concerned her was her husband, then her sons and daughters.

She wasn't yet twenty when she gave birth to her firstborn, Qasem. She saw his face before her and felt a stab of pain in her breast. Even though he had not yet turned thirty-five, he had gone bald before his time, and in the last three years his face had been taken over by wrinkles making him look twenty years older. Her second son, Hameed, was three years younger than

17

his brother. Unlike his brother, he had stuck to his studies and managed to finish secondary school before he was taken away for military service. He had spent two and a half years away from home. The same thing had happened with her youngest son, Saleh. It was a solace to her that all three of them were fortunate to marry women of the right sort, and grandchildren had sprung up all around her. The same went for her daughters Zahra and Hasna, whose husbands had joined the family.

Good Omen trots along at a lively pace. "Whenever you feel hungry or thirsty we can head to the fields," she tells him. Perhaps the swing of his head indicates he's understood. She takes some time to listen to the silence within herself. Her husband had died before he was yet sixty. Some men live to see eighty, others ninety. Her sorrow spreads inside her chest. She wishes she could make him hear her. "Why did you abandon me?" It occurs to her to alert Good Omen. "Don't forget…" She stays still for a few seconds, as if to make sure he was listening closely. "We go to Bu Qasem's resting place between the two palm trees, before continuing on to Sabiliyat."

They follow their route alongside the palm tree groves while giving them some berth. In the early morning of the first day, she walked for four hours without a break before pausing to rest for an hour next to a grassy patch, which afforded Good Omen a delicious meal. She continued her progress for another four hours, and then she decided to rest for two hours and took a little nap. She divided up the evening of her first day into two shifts, three hours each. After the darkness had enveloped everything, she settled down for the night on a grassy hill overlooking the Euphrates.

- 2 -

"WHAT DO YOU THINK, GOOD OMEN?" Good Omen was busy chewing at some of the juicy grasses in the vicinity. He raised his head a little. Had he heard her?

"Will we make it to Bu Qasem's grave tomorrow?" At that moment, Good Omen felt a powerful urge to lift his head high, stretch out his neck, and deliver an unchecked bray. But remembering her warning, he let out a controlled snort, which Um Qasem interpreted her own way. "That's what I thought," she said with satisfaction.

Bu Qasem had visited her dreams that night. "I'm happy you've decided to visit my grave," he told her. She rejoiced in her heart. "This won't be a short visit." Bu Qasem considered her words. "I don't follow." The decision came to her. "I will do anything not to leave you out there on your own." Without pausing he complained, "You returning to Sabiliyat worries me." "You have no reason to worry," she insisted. "The place isn't safe." "What place is?" she found herself asking antagonistically. "It's an area of military operations and civilians are not allowed to enter—" "This is the first time I hear you taking the government line," she interrupted him. His mouth opened as if he were about to speak, but nothing came out. A strange sound filtered inside her that seemed to be coming from behind her somewhere. She turned around to look. The rest of her dream faded away as she woke up to the sound of braying coming from far off.

The lights of dawn were beginning to spread in the east. She turned around in every direction, trying to spot Good Omen. He was nowhere in sight. Her heart began to thump. Had she made the biggest mistake of all when she neglected to tie him up by her side? A heavy wave of sadness washed over her, accompanied by a sudden sense of having fallen short. She slumped down helplessly. What should she do now? For a moment she was at a loss. The next moment she heard his snorting, as if he was telling her, "I'm here." Joy flooded over her. "So it was you braying," she answered, putting two and two together. Good Omen made no reply. Instead, he bent over the grass to sniff around, perhaps he'd find something tasty. A sense of vitality coursed through her, and she sprang to her feet. "We must keep going."

As they made their way briskly toward the South, she confided apologetically, "Sometimes suspicion is a sin." Had he understood her? "I woke up and didn't see you there and got it in my head you'd run away." A little while later she told him, "Bu Qasem visited me in my dreams." Hearing the name of his absent caretaker, Good Omen gave a snort and tossed his head. "He said he wasn't happy being where he was, in that grave in the middle of nowhere, and I promised not to leave him there." She was silent for a brief moment, and then she mused out loud, "What can be done about that, I wonder?"

A little before sunset on the second day, she noticed a dirt track slicing through the fields. Following it, she came across a young farmer weeding his field. She climbed off the donkey and called out a greeting. The young man lifted his head, gazing up at the stranger.

"How much longer is it to Nasiriya?"

The farmer reflected for a moment.

"If you keep going another ten minutes, you'll reach the edge of the international highway."

She listened attentively.

"If you were to take a taxi you'd be in Nasiriya in an hour."

She didn't say, *What if I didn't take a taxi?*—figuring he'd noticed the donkey.

"In your situation now…" his voice trailed off, "you'll need a whole day."

She was thinking she might make her way alongside the international highway, but she worried what would happen if she ran into a military patrol or reconnaissance unit who might question her: *"Where are you heading?…"*

"Where will you be spending the night?" the young man asked sympathetically.

A deep sigh escaped her, and her husband's words came back to her—"God's land is big enough for everyone, my son."

"You can spend the night in my house."

She was startled by the young man's offer.

He pointed in the distance. "Our village is only a few minutes away. My wife would be pleased to have you as her guest."

Um Qasem was at a loss how to respond. Her entire life she had never been in this kind of situation before. Did she have a right to decline his invitation? Her body went numb all over. She remembered she was in need of a wash, having slept on the ground the night before. It flashed through her mind that she should reply with a heartfelt *I don't wish to be a burden*. But instead, she accepted his offer.

"May God reward your kindness."

They walked along side by side followed by Good Omen, who didn't waste the opportunity to nibble away at the tips of the grasses along the path. The young man couldn't disguise his astonishment.

"What if your donkey ran away?"

"He has no reason to," she answered calmly.

Her confidence made him smile. "My name is Saleh," he said.

Her face lit up. "That's the name of my youngest son. He's around your age." Her presence of mind returning, she introduced herself. "I'm Um Qasem."

After a few moments' silence Saleh asked, "How did you get here?"

Finding it difficult to answer his question directly, she said, "I've come from Najaf."

The young man returned earnestly, "God preserve those who call on the Prophet's family."

"I'm going to visit my husband's grave," she explained.

He seemed interested in hearing more, and she felt no uneasiness relating the story to him. The unexpected timing of her husband's death...it had been more than two years ago, yet that searing sense of loss still ate away at her. Then one day the conviction had dawned—*her house in Sabiliyat would be able to hold her.*

"What's 'Sabiliyat'?" Saleh asked her curiously.

That was the name of the village where Um Qasem had

been born and where she'd lived all her life…

Saleh's wife was surprised for a moment to see her husband returning in the company of a woman, but it didn't take long for her to grasp the situation.

"God preserve those who visit our home."

She noticed with interest how quickly her child, who wasn't yet a year old, took to the newcomer, wrapping its arms around Um Qasem's neck as if they had known each other a long time. At that instant, her husband leaned in and whispered into his wife's ear, "A god-fearing woman coming from the holy shrines."

Wishing to forestall any anxiety the young couple might have that she would take advantage of their generosity, Um Qasem said, "I won't impose on you for long." Then to be clear, she added, "I'll be leaving at dawn."

When Saleh led him to the pen where the animals were kept, Good Omen became unbearably distressed at the sight of a gigantic cow with bulging horns, which met him with dark looks. He'd been in frays with his own kind before, and a donkey would use its hind legs to land a kick on its opponent, leaving time to prepare or flee. But cows attack by thrusting at you with their head, horns and all. Good Omen waited until Saleh had left the pen, and then he followed him out and posted himself in the dusty courtyard not far from the door of the house. He was surprised to hear Saleh addressing him. "If you insist…" With a wave of his hand, he disappeared inside the pen and returned carrying a bale of grass and a bucket of water.

When the sun rose the next morning, Um Qasem and

Good Omen were speeding along toward the South alongside the international highway. Um Qasem kept glancing at the rows of date palms on her left. With luck on her side, she'd be able to find the spot with the two date palms standing aloof where her husband was buried. While he was still alive, she used to claim she knew a lot of things about him. On the other hand, now that he'd left her for all eternity, she was less sure…But since he'd gone away, he'd made a practice of visiting her in her dreams. To be able to see him despite their separation was a partial compensation.

Her thoughts flew back to the days of her youth. She'd been her parents' only child. The house she'd grown up in stood in the middle of a sprawling date palm plantation belonging to the Naqeeb family, located on the western end of the village of Sabiliyat. In the middle of the plantation was a cemetery that had been abandoned many decades since. People called it the Ezz Al-Deen Cemetery, a reference to the shrine of a pious man by that name whose four walls still stood there. Her father worked as a foreman of the farmhands for the Naqeebs. She remembers their house, made up of a spacious hut with a thatched roof for receiving guests, a smaller one where her parents slept, and a hut with adobe walls for her.

She was seventeen when she first set eyes on her husband. He had come around with his donkeys to transport some dates from the area behind the house where they used to store them to the spot where the wooden skiffs docked on Chouma River. Maybe they exchanged glances at first without meaning, maybe she started looking for pretexts to come out of the house whenever he was around. Soon after the date harvest was over, he turned up to ask for her hand. Her father's words at the time crowd her mind all over again. "He's a fine young man, and we have a family connection through his father, who comes from Al-Ahsa." Even though it made her jump for joy inside, she wouldn't have had the power to say no in any case. Marriage was a matter for her father and her mother to decide.

The engagement period lasted two months. She remembers how much the wedding preparations had engrossed her mother and her. Two weeks after they were married, her husband took her parents and her on a trip to the holy shrines. That was at the beginning of 1946. At the beginning of 1948, she gave birth to her first son, Qasem. Sons and daughters followed in quick succession. After the birth of her youngest daughter Hasna, Um Qasem prayed to the Lord to seal her womb so she wouldn't get pregnant again, as a mercy to her husband and to ease the struggle for their worldly needs. God answered her prayers.

At the beginning of 1958, her father came down with a fever from which he did not recover. Her father's death did not surprise Um Qasem. Human life is in God's hands. What bewilders her to this day was what happened to her mother after her father died. She was plunged into something like a state of constant distraction, which she would occasionally break out of to exclaim "Here I am!" as if responding to someone's call. An anguished feeling would then come over her, wrestling with a sense of disorientation. "What is it, Mother?" "I heard your father's voice summoning me," she would answer with distress.

Her mother died a year after her father, after contracting a similar kind of fever.

The blow Um Qasem had suffered by losing her husband was also an event of a monumental order, regardless of whether it happened when it did or whether it had waited a couple more years. But fundamentally, it was different from what her mother had experienced. Should she put it down to the sense of connection between two beings who had grown so used to being together that when one left, the other was unable to go on living?

Good Omen's steps grew heavier after two hours of brisk exertion. The thought flashed through her mind that it must be the hardness of the ground along the highway and the din of cars going by. "You have a point," she said to him with understanding, mixed with remorse. She dismounted and looked around. To the right of the road, she spotted a thicket of reeds where the ground made a light dip, only a couple of minutes' walk away. "What do you say we head over?" In a flash he had bolted, and she was forced to raise her voice. "I'm not a young girl anymore, able to keep up with you." Reaching the thicket, she saw a mass of reeds and grasses rising out of a sunken bit of ground. It was covered with water that drained out of a neighboring pond. Good Omen was standing amid the stalks of reed, chewing at the tips of some grasses. She approached with caution. She bent over the water, scooped some up in her palm, and brought it to her mouth. She gargled it in her mouth a few times to determine whether it was good to drink or brackish, and it felt right to let it go down. "It's safe for you to drink," she said. She knew him well. When he wished to express his approval, he gave an obedient toss of the head.

After sunset she was able make out the yellow lights of the city of Nasiriya on the edge of the horizon to the South. Her heart began to race. Would she soon get the chance to speak to her husband up close? She would sit facing his grave and address her words to him. She would chide him for his cruelty in going away so soon. She might also tell him—why not—about how his extended family, his sons and daughters and grandchildren, were now living close to the holy shrines.

She heaved out a sorrowful sigh and addressed herself to Good Omen. "We must find the two date palms where..." She didn't finish her sentence. She had the sense that Good Omen had understood her. He picked up pace. She remembered distinctly that the two date palms where her husband had been buried stood right next to one another and were nearly the same height, so that their leaves intermeshed.

Grey clouds gathered in the sky, cloaking the stars and making the darkness deepen. The fact that she could see the lights of the city of Nasiriya in the distance didn't mean that there was light where she was standing. Her vision blurred as she looked at the date palms. All of them seemed to be nearly the same height, with intermeshing leaves. Her aching head grew heavy. "You must be tired, too." Good Omen made a low snort. "I'm tired," she went on plaintively. He turned his steps toward a nearby hill. "Since you chose this spot..." There was gratitude in her voice. She picked a clean bit of ground, spread out her blanket, and nestled her head on her arm. Maybe her headache would stop if she could get some rest, away from the din of the passing cars. Good Omen drifted about nearby grazing. Sleep eluded her. She kept tossing and turning on her blanket.

It was three in the morning when she woke up to the sense of something cold pattering against her face. She realized that a light drizzle had begun to fall from a cluster of clouds passing overhead. It struck her as a good sign. Good Omen emitted a few low snorts welcoming the drops of rain. He drew closer and kneeled at her feet. "You're a good one," she said to him. After a few minutes the cluster of clouds dispersed, and the pale silver light of millions of stars hung over everything. She felt a drowsy weight beginning to play on her eyelids, and she surrendered to sleep for a second time.

How is it she could hear the voice of her son Hameed calling her? She knew it was three whole days since she'd left her family behind. She ebbed and flowed in her slumber until consciousness swept back over her. She opened her eyes and saw him leaning over her.

"Mother!"

A flooding joy made her heart skip. She sat up instantly and pulled him to her breast. She caught sight of her sons Qasem and Saleh standing at her feet. She spread her arms. Should she ask her sons, *"How did you find me?"* As she was getting up, she noticed a taxi idling close by.

"We'd given up hope of finding you," Qasem told her. "We entered Basra, we got to the area of Ma'qil, but then the army wouldn't let us continue south. We had to spend the night in Al-Zubayr hoping we'd get to Sabiliyat, but there were soldiers everywhere. We retraced our steps feeling disheartened, and while we were driving past, Saleh spotted Good Omen."

She turned around to give her donkey a grateful look. He felt happy to be surrounded by so many of his caretakers, but his happiness was incomplete. Why hadn't they brought along the other donkeys?

They began to plead with her. "Come back with us."

"There are two issues here…" she trailed off.

"What's the first?" asked her son Hameed.

"I need to find the place where your father is buried."

28

"It's a stone's throw away," he replied. "We stopped by a short while ago," he added. "There, you see those facing palm trees?" He pointed.

She squinted in that direction. A burst of energy coursed through her limbs. "I will go to him." She raised her voice. "Good Omen!"

Her son Saleh called her back. "What about the second issue?"

"You'll hear it when the time comes," she replied tersely.

Um Qasem was the first to reach the grave. She opened to him with a greeting. "You know how much I love you and worry about you." She listened closely for a moment as if waiting for a response before going on. "I will do as you asked: I won't leave you here."

When her sons had caught up with her, she said to them, "It's making your father unhappy to be lying here in the middle of nowhere. He doesn't want to stay here."

Her sons exchanged conspiratorial glances.

"What are you scheming about?" she asked them.

Saleh was quick to answer. "We've agreed to come back with a religious man sometime later and transfer his remains to the Najaf graveyard."

Her mind fell still as she heard their decision. "Why don't we recover his remains now?" she proposed.

Her sons exchanged glances again. They were amazed to discover their mother's mind was working in a way that flouted every convention. She didn't let them wallow in their confusion long. She pointed at the horizon to where the city of Nasiriya shaded into view. "One of you can take the taxi and go bring a religious man," she said.

Her eldest son Qasem stepped up. "I'll go."

"We'll need a shovel and a white cloth," someone else pointed out.

It took Qasem two hours to return, accompanied by a religious man. Cautiously they dig. They are astonished to find the body had decomposed. All that's left are the bones of the hands and feet, parts of the spinal cord, and the skull.

After the religious man had recited the verses from the Qur'an and the invocations he explained, "The body of the deceased decomposed because of groundwater seeping in from the salt marsh."

The sons hastened to gather what remained of their father and folded it up inside the shroud. The religious man said to them in condolence, "You do honor to the deceased by taking him to Najaf's noble graveyard."

Um Qasem was swift to spring her question. "What if the departed had given instructions to be buried in his birthplace?"

The religious man didn't need to think. "The will of the deceased is binding."

"Oh Mother."

"Oh Mother."

"Oh Mother…" echoed the appeals of Qasem, Hameed and then Saleh.

"You are all in my heart," she said to her sons, "but my soul and the soul of your departed father will only find rest in Sabiliyat."

"Where did you come up with this birthplace business?" her youngest son Saleh asked.

"That's what your father said to me two nights ago."

"Only madmen—!" her eldest nearly blurted out.

She realized which way his thoughts were turning. "When the war is over, you'll come home and find your mother waiting for you."

A sense of helplessness overcame them. They took turns heaping warnings on her. "You're proposing to enter an area of military operations that is off limits for civilians."

"Don't you worry about me," she said to them.

"We can't let you go just like that," they pleaded.

She smiled at them tenderly. "You can come with me if you wish."

Was it shock that robbed them of the power of speech and made their tongues cling to their throats?

She embraced them one by one. "Look after yourselves." She didn't notice her son Qasem slipping a few banknotes into her pocket. She hugged the cloth that contained the remains of her husband's bones to her chest.

"We must continue our journey, Good Omen."

Her donkey began eagerly toward the South, while her sons bade her farewell with despondent looks. After she'd gone a little way, she turned around and saw them still standing there. She waved at them. "I'll be seeing you…"

- 3 -

IF SOMEONE WERE TO ASK HER point-blank, *"What are you hiding in that bundle you've got to your chest?"* her nerve would fail her. *"What's left of my husband's dead body,"* she'd say. They would immediately think, *"This woman has lost it."* After he had died, they had hastily carried out the burial rites and resumed their journey north. At the time, she was gripped by an overpowering sense of loss. Even so, the idea of moving his remains hadn't yet crossed her mind until he'd entered her dreams, telling her how unhappy he was to be lying buried in that cold place in the middle of nowhere. The truth was that she couldn't have explained to anyone in so many words what use it was for her to be carrying his bones now. It was simply this sense of having in her possession something that was intimately hers and knowing she could speak to him whenever she wished. One thing was certain, he no longer had any excuse for not visiting her regularly at night.

Her mind flies back to the claim she'd made to her family when the idea of transferring his remains to the Najaf graveyard came up. "He gave instructions to be buried in his birthplace," she'd told them. It was her desperate desire to stay together with him, no matter what it took. To make up for that claim, she promised him she'd do her best to convey to her

32

sons the following instructions: "After I join your father, you may transfer both of our remains to the graveyard in Najaf."

She continued her progress south. The planted fields kept following the horizon on her left. She decided to divide her time into shifts. She wouldn't have known how far they'd gone into the night were it not for the steady rhythm of Good Omen's hoofbeats. She couldn't say for sure that he was in the best shape. She needed to have feeling for the limits of this poor creature that had her in his care. She turned around searching and spotted a thicket. "Let's head over." Good Omen responded with enthusiasm. A spurt of energy shot through his hooves, and he burst into a gallop. One of the best things about Um Qasem was the way she could read his thoughts.

After two days of fast-paced travel, she began to notice a significant buildup of activity from military vehicles of various kinds, ranging from military Jeeps and troop carriers of different sizes to oversized multiwheel trucks carrying massive tanks and cannons. At the same time, the number of passenger cars slowed to a trickle. She had entered the province of Basra. The idea that she was now only a short distance from the site of military battles didn't make her anxious. What preoccupied her more was the possibility of being stopped by one of their patrol units and questioned, *"Where are you going?"* How would she respond if she was confronted with statements like *"This is a zone of active military operations"* or *"Entry is forbidden to civilians."* Her only option was to try to stay out of sight, since being seen meant being subjected to humiliating interrogation, followed by inevitable expulsion. Her imagination careened.

What would happen to Good Omen if the army came across her and decided to detain her? She spent a long time turning things over in her mind.

She continued south by crossing into the palm tree plantations to the west of the Shatt al-Arab near where the desert began, not far from a wide road that had been recently paved, which ran from the Bab Al-Zubayr junction all the way down to the port of Al-Faw on the coast of the Gulf. Before the evacuation, it had been a narrow winding road. They had since widened it and done their utmost to straighten it out to make it easier for their gigantic machines to move up and down. She'd strain her ears in every direction, and whenever she picked up the rumble of an engine she'd slip in among the palm trees and stay hidden there until the danger had passed. Good Omen caught on to the delicacy of the situation and began to accelerate toward the interior of the plantations the moment he felt Um Qasem jabbing him with her heel or whispering a warning.

On the evening of the third day, she was forced to hide with Good Omen behind a small hill inside one of the orchards because military vehicles kept going up and down the road every few minutes. Night fell. She noticed they didn't have their headlights on. The hours rolled by. Drowsiness overcame her, and she surrendered to sleep. She saw her husband before her, standing at the door of their house. She felt the urge to ask him what had kept him so long, to scold him. "It's not like you to disappear just like that and not care about what happens to me. If that's the way it has to be, then take me with you." She had a sudden conviction that he was smiling at her. She felt his hand reaching out to look for hers and gave it to him. She heard him whispering to her, "You're tiring yourself out more than you should be." She replied, "Your presence alone is enough to—" She wasn't able to finish her sentence. He faded from view, leaving behind only the feel of his hand in her palm.

The sound of low snorts drifted to her from nearby, and she opened her eyes. She was lying on her back looking at the dawn sky while Good Omen hovered near where her head was resting. "I must have slept a while," she explained apologetically. She reassured herself that the bundle containing her husband's bones was still there before getting up. She listened attentively in every direction. No sign of the rumble of military vehicles. She heard the cooing of a pigeon somewhere nearby. She studied her surroundings—Basran country, as only it could be. Whole fields of palm trees shading into each other as though they formed a single cultivation, that extraordinary mesh of thousands of streams and ponds created by the ebb and flow of water.

Her intuition tells her she isn't far from home. If she kept going now, she might be able to make it there by late afternoon. Taking into account the obstacles posed by the military vehicles passing by, she could make it there by nightfall. Her heart had begun to thump. The warm feeling of being at home, the familiar smells of things. But then, suppose the army gets wind of an unauthorized person being in the area, they kick their way in and ask, *"Who are you?"* How would she justify her presence? Her mind quickening, she formulates another question that someone or other is bound to put to her sooner or later: *"How did you get here without being stopped by any of our security checkpoints?"* A weary smile of resignation traces itself on her face...everything in its own time.

35

"Time to get going," she said, turning to Good Omen. She climbed onto his back. There was no need for her to show him the way. He began speeding toward the South. After an hour's travel, the leaves of the palm trees changed color. They were now yellow, as far as the eye could see. She noticed sawgrass growing everywhere, a sign of neglect. Suddenly, Good Omen gave a start and then Um Qasem did too, before she could ask, "What's wrong?" He snorted in protest. She noticed something darting through a clump of sawgrass nearby and then spotted the head of a dusty-looking wild boar beating a hasty retreat. These sprawling fields had been standing deserted for a while. Wild animals had come in and made their nests, and their numbers had multiplied, making up for the absence of human beings. The facts speak for themselves. The possibility of there being wolves in the area couldn't be ruled out either.

She leaned forward a little and whispered, "What do you think, Good Omen?" He didn't respond with a toss of his head. Instead, he started moving along again at a steady tempo and her spirits settled a little, knowing he would sense danger before it struck. She noticed that the ponds and creeks had run dry. Water doesn't dry up for no reason. The war alone wouldn't stop the Shatt al-Arab from flowing. A sense of apprehension suddenly seized her. *I want to see the Shatt. I hope no unimaginable evil has come to it.* "Let's head for the Shatt, making sure we keep out of the army's sight," she said to Good Omen.

Instead of continuing their course toward the South, they veered east, crossing into the date palm groves with their faded leaves. From time to time, Good Omen would give a low snort of warning, signaling the presence of some animal in the vicinity. Um Qasem had no time to feel afraid, but just to be on the safe side she took out her sickle, snapped off a branch from a mulberry tree, and sharpened its tip. After going for two hours, she caught sight of the road of Abul Khaseeb, which sliced through the fields of date palms and took in dozens of villages along its course. "Shsh," she whispered to Good Omen. Good Omen stood stock-still. She strained her ears toward the road. No sign of rumbling trucks or human voices. She heard a raven caw. Good Omen swung his head. "Now don't you bray," she reminded him. He contented himself with a low snort like a snore. She climbed off his back and instructed him, "Wait for me here. I won't be long."

She crossed the asphalt road with a brisk stride and entered the grove of date palms on the opposite side. The Shatt al-Arab wasn't far off, she was sure of it. She felt a fresh gust of wind on her face coming from the east and noticed the damp musty scent of the Shatt. She breathed a sigh of relief. It's still here, they couldn't put an end to it. A few minutes passed and she heard the low mutter of men's voices. She quickly stepped behind the trunk of a palm tree and paused to listen. The muttering voices continued. Using one of the dried-up creeks for camouflage, she approached the Shatt, stepping cautiously for a few minutes. The dampness and the soughing of water grew stronger, and so did the muttering voices. Getting up her courage, she lifted her head. She was surprised to see a number of small tents of faded khaki, the color of tree branches. A few soldiers were loitering near the tents. She saw the Shatt al-Arab churning with turquoise waters in the backdrop and felt a sense of peace returning. She turned around and retraced her steps.

As soon as he caught sight of her, Good Omen gave a welcoming swish of his tail. She thought she'd share with him what she'd learned. "Our Shatt is brimming with water, but the creeks are dry." She climbed onto his back. "Let's keep going." He broke into a trot. "You know the way to Sabiliyat."

They wove their way deep inside the fields to avoid running into the army. An hour later, she noticed a clearing ahead where the sky was visible through the leaves. It had to mean she was getting close to one of the main rivers. Good Omen sped up before coming to a halt at the rim of a steep ditch. Um Qasem looked around in every direction, hoping to find a way to identify this river that the long absence of water had transformed into an enormous trench, appearing as if out of nowhere. She jogged her memory. Along the Shatt al-Arab, between Al-Ashar and Sabiliyat, there were five big rivers—Al-Khoura, Al-Saraji, Muhaijran, Hamdan, and finally Hebaba. She knew she'd passed the fields watered by Al-Khoura River when she'd made her way along the outer bend of the strip of farmland right where the desert began. She racked her thoughts. If her instinct wasn't failing her, she had to be standing in front of Al-Saraji River.

Her gaze soaked it all in, the river and its bank, matted with reeds and papyrus plants. Part of the riverbed was cracked over from lack of water, while here and there one could see a few isolated spots containing pockets of water and patches of mud. The opposite bank was likewise covered in reeds and papyrus plants. An involuntary sigh escaped her. "What do you think?" she asked. Good Omen gave a snort. He approached the sloping arm of the river and began to pick his way down, steadying himself with his hooves. "You're doing well," she encouraged him. After he'd reached the riverbed, Good Omen had some difficulty scaling the opposite bank, and she had to dismount.

He seized the opportunity to start chewing at the tips of some papyrus plants. "Take your time," she reassured him.

She made it to the top of the steep slope and took a few steps around. Her body too needed to rest. She stretched herself out on the ground. The sky over Basra no longer looked the way it used to. There was a dullness about it that made her spirit clench. She knew it was a time of war, but she couldn't see why they had to destroy everything that blooms by making the rivers run dry. *If your enemy is stationed deep inside his country, which lies behind the Shatt al-Arab to the east, why must you destroy every living thing inside your own country, which lies right behind you to the west?*

After an hour they reached another trench. It was Muhaijran River. If only she knew how they'd managed to make these large rivers dry up. It was another half hour before they reached a third trench, Hamdan River. Her dismay deepened as she passed along an orchard that used to be planted with fruit trees. Twisted dry stalks were turning a brownish black. This used to be grapevine trellises in her time. Where the apricot, orange, apple, and lemon trees once stood, there were only bare ashen sticks. The banana trees had slumped to the ground like heaps of brown rags. She gazed up at the dull yellow leaves of the date palm trees. She knew date palms have formidable powers of endurance. Stroking her husband's bones, she let him in on her bewilderment. "How will we live in this desolation?" She caught sight of a thicket of reeds and papyrus plants. Good Omen's footsteps grew slower until he finally ground to a halt. She dismounted. "You must be hungry." With a quick toss of his head, he made for the thicket.

Her heart skipped a beat the moment she came up to the dry trench of Hebaba River. She couldn't suppress her excitement. "We're almost there." Good Omen broke into a gallop. "Don't overdo it," she pleaded, and he slowed down again. "We have to be careful, we might run into the army. They'll ask, *'Where have you come from?'* And even if they take pity on Um Qasem's grey hair they might say, *'Go back where you came from, Old Woman, before you get hauled off and interrogated.'"*

A sense of conviction took hold of her. *If I get to my house and make it inside before any of them stop me, I'll know how to stay.* But the next moment she hesitated as she wondered to herself what would she say to them if they kicked their way into the house? She caressed the cloth containing her husband's bones. "God is our keeper."

The sun had disappeared behind the fields of palm trees to the west. She turned to Good Omen. "Let's hurry to Ezz Al-Deen's shrine and take shelter there." The sun had set when they reached their destination. She studied her surroundings. The farm workers' huts that used to stand in the vicinity had vanished without a trace. Her eyes made out a broad dirt track that rolled out in a straight line all the way to the edge of the desert. The army must have cleared a road for their vehicles. She climbed off Good Omen's back and outlined her plan to him. "I'll bed down by the wall of the shrine and get some rest until it's time for us to head to the house," she said decisively. Then she pointed to the palm trees and added, "You can go get a bite to eat." Good Omen trotted away and disappeared into the palm trees. She strained her ears listening for sounds in the distance. No sign of the rumble of engines. She breathed a sigh of satisfaction and moved quickly to bed down by the wall farthest from the road.

She wasn't able to doze off as she'd hoped. Her heart was in turmoil, weighed down by the sorrow of seeing landmarks disappear that had been so enmeshed with the life she'd lived there, in the place where she'd been born and spent her early years before Bu Qasem came to whisk her away. Her imagination took her to the center of the village. The huts of the farm workers, the pens where the animals were kept, the children's shouts. Her house was no more than a few minutes away, but what if those soldiers had set up their tents in the vicinity? Who knew whether they had turned her village into a military bunker. Thoughts kept pouring in until she began to scold herself. She hadn't even gotten there, it was too early to start worrying.

The deep enveloping silence soothed her spirits. It suddenly occurred to her that she should make use of the opportunity to honor her husband's bones by paying a visit to the saint's tomb. She went around the surviving chamber of the shrine and stopped before the entrance. The darkness gathered deeply inside. *"In the name of God, the compassionate, the merciful."* She crossed the threshold. Her senses picked up a fragrance like that of old incense. Gradually her eyes grew accustomed to the darkness. She made out the rectangular form of the tomb standing in the middle of the room. There were bits of cloth draped over it whose color she couldn't distinguish just then, but which she knew to be green. Some people in Sabiliyat kept a practice of making pledges to Ezz Al-Deen, and these pledges would always include a drape, which would be replaced from one year to the next. She took a few steps toward the rectangular tomb, held out the bundle with the bones, and set it down on top. "One thing I know about you,

Bu Qasem, is that you have a great love for Ezz Al-Deen."
Collecting herself, she recited the opening sura of the Qur'an.
She then sat down on the floor and propped her back against
the tomb. A sense of peace washed over her, which she had
missed for a long time.

How can a person travel dozens of years back in time
while still remaining in the present? She was a young girl, and
suddenly there was her mother, coming to confide in her. "Bu
Qasem has come to ask for your hand." She wasn't surprised to
hear her mother using that name to refer to the man she hadn't
married yet, later to bear him a son called Qasem. Getting up
her courage, she said to her mother, "I love him." Her mother
stared at her in astonishment, but this didn't prevent her from
continuing, "And he loves me back." Her mother made as if
to reprimand her, but she went on, "I want him to be my
husband." Clinching the point, she added, "It's enough that he
trusted me with his bones."

At the word "bones," she felt her ribs pressing in on her.
A treacherous awareness came back to her. Bu Qasem was no
longer alive, her mother was no longer. She stopped breathing.
If she could cry, she might be able to relieve the devastation
she felt at that moment. At the same moment, the full daylight
of consciousness swept over her, the point where a person's
endurance breaks down, confronted by dreams with a power
greater than reality. Suddenly her body gave a violent shudder,
and she found herself beginning to wail inconsolably.

After a few minutes, the sound of Good Omen's muffled
snorts reached her. It must be his way of letting her know he
was standing at the entrance. She struggled to her feet and

hugged the cloth with the bones tightly. "You're a good one," she said to Good Omen. Stillness pervaded unbroken all around her. The nights used to be filled with the croaking of frogs. The drying-out of the rivers must have made the frogs migrate, or die off en masse. She lifted her head. The sky was bursting with stars. She turned her gaze toward the east. She had about two hours left before the morning dawned. She should make the most of the darkness. "Let's go home," she said to Good Omen as she climbed onto his back. To her surprise he broke into a gallop. "Don't go too fast," she begged him.

Following the dirt track for ten minutes, they reached the road of Abul Khaseeb, not far from where Maude Bridge crossed over the river Sayyid Rajab. "Shshsh." She strained to listen. There was nothing in the air that would indicate the presence of human beings. She dismounted and walked up to the bridge. She bent over to look at the riverbed, nourishing a hope she might see the stars shining back on the surface of the water. She felt a constriction in her chest. There was just a muddy trench resembling all the other rivers she'd met on her way. She was surprised to hear herself saying adamantly, "Everywhere but here." To her mind, Sabiliyat was the one place that could never suffer the fate of dying from lack of water. But the reality before her made her heart sink.

She felt a bitter taste collecting under her tongue. If it was up to her, she'd have the waters of the Shatt al-Arab flowing freely down the rivers that veined out of it. Her eyes followed Abul Khaseeb Road into the distance. A few minutes more and she'd be at the houses of Sabiliyat. "Let's go."

Good Omen obeyed instantly and started trotting along ahead of her. "Only remember, no braying," she reminded him.

- 4 -

BEING NEAR IS ALMOST LIKE being there already, the hunger, the yearning to melt into a place and be one with it. Her heart was swelling, her stride had lengthened, she had to stop herself from running. Good Omen met speed with speed. There was the old tamarisk tree standing at the top of the road that leads into the village. Some people thought it not right for a desert tamarisk to be growing among the groves of date palms, but it's the hallmark of the village of Sabiliyat. Bu Qasem said to her one day, "This tamarisk tree has been standing here since the day I was born. It's at least a hundred and fifty years old." In the days of the Ottoman Empire, someone from the Naqeeb family decided to attach three big water jars to the trunk of the tree so it could serve as a fountain for travelers.

Her thoughts cascading, she remembered that it had been hours since Good Omen had had a drop of water. With the effort he'd exerted, he had to be extremely thirsty. The tributary rivers being all dry, she'd have to aim for the main source. The Shatt al-Arab was a quarter of an hour's trek from where they stood. The question was whether to take Good Omen there first or stop by her house to have a look around. She suddenly noticed that Good Omen was now bounding ahead. "Don't go too fast," she said to him. But he continued rushing forward, letting out a muffled snort as he went. She couldn't be angry. His sudden spurt of energy might be an irresistible yearning for his first home.

She gazed into the distance. The paved road ran in a straight line from Maude Bridge, with its cement frame, to the wooden bridge on Chouma River before turning right in the direction of the village called Bab Al-Hawa. The names of things, what they stood for… People in these parts understood things by the names they gave them. To her right, shielded from view by the remains of a mud wall, lay a date palm orchard called Al-Daleeshiya, which took its name from its owner, Hajj Jawad Al-Daleeshi.

She strained her ears hoping she might pick up some sound signaling the presence of life, any life. The deep silence had a ring all its own. On cultivated land, the nights are normally abuzz with different kinds of sounds, the frogs, the blackbeetles. Silence meant land that's barren. An explanation came to her. *Unless it's the war that's caused this.* The senselessness of her own conclusion made her mind stop. Everyone knows what war means. It means deafening noise, guns being fired, cannons discharging, planes dropping bombs. Her mind paused again. She realized that during her trek she hadn't heard any cannons going off or planes roaring overhead. Perhaps they'd gotten tired of their war. Or maybe they were up to something she had no way of guessing.

Here was the old tamarisk tree. She couldn't stop herself from reaching out to stroke its trunk, grown stony over the years. She was now at the top of the main street of Sabiliyat. The contours of the road stood out hazily in the dark. Before the evacuation, there used to be a dim yellow light coming

45

from lanterns fixed to the top of the electricity poles. The circumstances of war require total darkness. She stopped short for a moment. Up to this point there had been nothing to give cause for worry. She cautiously moved forward. These were the shadows of her house, the large hut that served as a pen for the animals and the row of rooms that mushroomed after her sons and daughters got married.

Her steps had quickened of their own accord. She had been expecting to find Good Omen standing by the door of the house. She saw the door was ajar. A cry almost escaped her but she managed to keep it back. *"I'm here!"* Her senses drank in the smell of stale dust. She dropped to her knees. The ferment in her heart was too much for her. She let herself sob freely for a few minutes before she eventually regained her composure. She felt amazed at her sons' and daughters' capacity to adjust to new places. For her part, she wasn't sure her reluctance was simply due to old age.

She raised her voice a little. "Good Omen?" She heard his muffled snort coming from the direction of the pen. "You must be thirsty." He emerged from the pen and came toward her. She struggled to her feet. She unbuckled the saddlebags and they slid off his back. He said thanks by a vigorous shake of his body. She reached out and stroked his forehead with the flat of her hand. "You're a good one." Her mind began to work...how to get water for Good Omen. If she were to leave him to his own devices he'd know his way to the water, but what with the dark and her fear of the army finding her out before she was ready to confront them...Her lips parted in a wry smile. *As if I'll ever be ready to confront them.* She turned to Good Omen and said, "Let's go to the Shatt." He complied with a snore.

They followed the road along toward the east. The only thing she could hear was the clopping of Good Omen's hooves on the asphalt. To her right was the wall that ran around the boys' primary school. In times gone by…the hours of the morning, the children shouting, the yellow light in the window of the room where the school guard Salman used to sit. She walked on, leaving the school behind. Silence crouched behind the closed doors of the houses. What good are houses once they've been abandoned by their people? They kept going and came to the building where the girls' school used to be housed. She felt a hollowness in her chest. Thirty years ago they had started offering evening classes for women, to eradicate illiteracy. At the time, she had been able to join the classes for six months, and she had picked up some of the letters of the alphabet and also learned to write her name.

She felt gusts of moist wind blowing into her face. It was the Shatt she knew so well, she was coming up to it. She was about to quicken her pace when she heard the sound of a man coughing. She froze to the spot as if she had turned to stone. The cough had come from the direction of the Shatt. "Shshsh," she whispered to Good Omen. He obeyed and stopped in his tracks. She strained to listen. The coughing came again.

"You should ask permission to visit the doctor."

"Just coughing won't earn you a medical report that gets you off the hook for military service," the other responded sarcastically.

The first one laughed. "Unless your coughing is from some serious contagious disease."

What gives them the right to take over the Shatt? Um Qasem asked herself indignantly. She whispered to Good Omen,

"Let's get away."

Good Omen uttered a low snort and turned to follow her.

She had no idea how the soldiers would react when they discovered her there. She thought it unlikely they'd open fire but kept an open mind about the possibility that they might place her under immediate arrest. After all, she had her defense: *"This is where I live."* Suppose they heard her out and argued back, *"You're risking your life inside an area of active military operations." "God is our keeper,"* would be her reply, and if they were still receptive she'd add, *"The life of a tired-out old woman isn't more valuable than the lives of young men like you."* She would come up with more arguments if the situation demanded. Her imagination sparred on. What if they forced her to leave without giving her a hearing, if one of those higher-ups barked out an order at her? *"Clear out immediately, or else!"*

She quickly waved the notion away. She had enough on her hands trying to find water for Good Omen. She remembered the watering spot on Chouma River that stood close to her house. That spot was so deep it could maintain a reservoir of water even when the tide was at its lowest during winter. "Let's go to our watering spot," she whispered to Good Omen. He submitted and followed her without making a sound.

As they reached the area, Um Qasem noticed that the day was beginning to break. Her heart started to thump. The arrival of daylight meant a greater chance of being found out by the army. She'd had a notion that there mightn't be any soldiers stationed in Sabiliyat, but now that she'd heard their voices… It seemed they were camped out not far from the bank of the Shatt, the way they were behind the bridge on Al-Saraji River.

She peered into the watering hole. Her intuition hadn't

48

failed her: there was some water left. Good Omen would be able to get his due and drink his fill. He steadied himself with his hooves as he made his way down to the hole. He bent over the water, sniffed at it, and then tossed his head disapprovingly. "The water's bad?" she wondered aloud. She approached the water, reached out, scooped up a palmful, and brought it to her nostrils. It had lain stagnant in muddy ground for a long time and had an acrid smell. She turned to Good Omen. "You have a point." She sighed, perplexed. What to do? Good Omen didn't linger. He began making his way back up the embankment. "Where are you going?" she called out. He kept going as if he hadn't heard her. "You won't be able to figure this out all on your own." She only objected because there might be no water to be found.

She hurried to her house after him and was cheered to see him standing expectantly next to the basin connected to a tap in the middle of the courtyard. "Those were the old days," she said to him with a sad sigh. She sensed he hadn't caught her drift, as he brought his snout to the knob and began to sniff at it. "You don't believe me," she chided him. He gave a toss of his head. "The tap has no water," she explained. He refused to budge. "Since you won't take no for an answer…" she said with a shrug and reached out to the tap and turned it, to prove what she'd said. A faint noise sputtered from the air that had been trapped inside for a while. Suddenly Um Qasem was astonished to see water jet out in strong bursts. She was overcome by laughter. "So you do know where to find water!"

As the morning light grew stronger, she had a chance to go through her house and check things over. Everything looked just as it had when she had left it, only lying under a thick coat of dust. Things lose their value when their owners go away. She could almost hear the voices of her sons and daughters calling out to her. *"Mother, where have you gone?"* Their voices merge into one and become a collective reproach. She turned and looked all around. Perhaps she'd made a mistake when she'd decided to leave them and go away.

Good Omen was no longer standing by the water basin. She had a feeling that he must also be suffering from loneliness, in his own way. The wind wafted over to her the distant sound of men murmuring. Anxiety seized her. It was only a matter of time. They would kick their way into the house. *"Who gave you permission? How did you get here?"* What will she reply? Her mind baulked, nothing coalesced in her imagination. She couldn't escape her fate, but she prayed to God that he lighten the load.

She hung back broodingly for a moment and then turned to the cloth bundle containing her husband's bones. "No harm in starting to prepare your grave." She cast a critical eye over the courtyard. The most suitable location was the spot where the ground rose right next to the Hilawi date tree. Their house had never lacked farming tools. She picked out a shovel. She had never had to dig a grave before. "I'm doing this for you, Bu Qasem," she said, trying to boost her resolve.

She spent the next two hours digging. The dug-out soil piling up around the pit slowly blocked out her surroundings. She didn't notice the sun had begun to shine more brightly in the courtyard. She paused to study the results of her work. It didn't seem like enough. A grave must be at least two meters deep, she found herself thinking.

She was so engrossed in her labors that she didn't notice the three soldiers who suddenly burst through the door into the courtyard.

"What are you doing here!"

When she heard the gruffness and hostility in the soldier's voice, her body gave a violent shudder. She raised her eyes and saw the muzzles of three machine guns pointed at her chest. "Who are you?" one of them hollered. The next thing she knew her will had failed her. Her body followed, and she slumped to the ground, unconscious.

Why hadn't Bu Qasem warned her while he had the chance...Good Omen with his keen hearing, what had prevented him from...Her thoughts washing over her in a tidal wave, the way they do when she feels helpless. A possibility occurred to her...

"Lady," someone was repeating urgently.

The voice reached her from the other side of the world. *Where am I?* she wondered as she struggled to gather herself.

"She's breathing."

"There's no reason she wouldn't."

"Has she come to?" a voice asked from farther off.

"It looks like she needs a bit more time, sir," came the reply from somewhere near.

Perhaps the presence of so many people talking over her head was too much for her, and her hand shot up as if to wave their voices away.

"She moved her hand!" one cried out joyfully.

A voice with greater authority came closer, and the others moved away a little. The decision threshed itself in her mind—she ought to know what was happening. Without wavering long, she opened her eyelids.

A young man in a well-cut military uniform was standing a couple of steps away. This had to be their commanding officer. A number of young soldiers were hovering around her. She looked up and saw a piece of sky shimmering through the foliage of a tall Lebbeck tree. *I'm not in my house,* the conclusion filtered through.

"Where am I?" she asked in a mumble.

"You're inside a military area," said the young officer. There was surprise in his voice. She tried to get her thoughts in order. She was digging away building a grave for her husband when…Her mind quickened.

"Where's Good Omen?" she asked with alarm. Baffled looks passed between them.

"What's good omen?"

At the same moment, she heard his snore coming from somewhere behind where they were all congregated. She turned toward the direction of the snore. One of the soldiers standing next to her stepped to the side to give her a clear view. It was trying for her to see her donkey tied up by one of his hooves.

"Why the rope?" she asked with displeasure. She was calmed by the young officer's command.

"Untether the donkey."

He turned to her and without trying to disguise his astonishment said, "Your donkey understands you."

"It's a donkey," she replied without even thinking.

The moaning of waves coming from the Shatt drifted around her. So they were camped right beside the river.

"How did you get here?" the commanding officer broke into her thoughts, still extremely astonished.

How could she reply to a question that would seal her expulsion? Like someone seeking a stay of execution, even a short one, she said in a way she hoped would come across as feeble, "Would it be possible to have a cup of tea?"

Annoyed, his voice rose, "What a strange request."

In the same feeble tone she replied, "It's been a week since I last…" She closed her eyelids and drew a long sighing breath. "I hope she doesn't faint again," she heard someone say nervously. Quickly she opened her eyes.

"I won't faint."

Her gaze traveled from one face to another.

"What happened?" she asked. "I was digging Bu Qasem's grave—"

"Who is Bu Qasem?" the commanding officer stopped her.

"How did I get here?" she asked, instead of replying.

One of the soldiers answered, "You were out cold and we brought you here to take care of you."

"Bring her some tea," the officer said as if yielding to the inevitable.

She sensed that he noticed the tremor in her hand as she brought the cup to her lips. He didn't try to hide his concern.

"When was the last time you had something to eat?"

Not letting the opportunity go to waste, she said, "I can't remember."

Their dark brown bread, which was hard as rock, became soft and melt-in-the-mouth delicious as soon as she'd soaked it for a few seconds in the hot lentil soup. She wolfed down two whole pieces, one after the other. Secretly, she followed the way the officer was observing her. He seemed gratified to see how heartily she was eating their food. For her part, there was only one thing she cared about—that they shouldn't force her to leave. What would become of her if they did?

The soldiers had dispersed and the commanding officer was the only one left.

"What's your name?"

"Um Qasem."

He reflected for a moment. "How old is your son Qasem?"

"Many years older than you."

He smiled. "He must be one of those who were evacuated."

"Yes," she went on, "he lives with the rest of my family in Najaf."

The surprise was plain in his voice. "Surely you didn't get here on the back of your donkey."

She nodded.

"What about your family? Do they know about your trip?"

"They found out about it afterwards."

"What do you mean?" he asked with evident curiosity.

Before making any revelations, Um Qasem thought she'd check to see if the conditions were right. "If you're interested in hearing the story…"

"I am," he said.

Encouraged by this, she proceeded to relate the events in a way that fit the situation.

"We packed up and set off like everyone else. Then Bu Qasem gave me a shock by passing away in his sleep." She was silent for a moment. "It wasn't right that he should go away without a word of farewell."

The young man's eyebrows shot up in surprise.

"We had just made it past the city of Nasiriya. So as to be able to identify his grave more easily, his sons decided to bury him between two date palms right next to the international highway." She could see he was listening closely. "There was no time for mourning rites, no time to grieve. All this had to be put off until we'd found someplace to settle."

She breathed in deeply and then heaved out a long sigh. "I have five children and nearly twenty grandchildren...I have only one Bu Qasem." She stole a glance at his face. The look of interest was still there. "We continued going until we made it to Najaf a few days later. We set up our shacks not far from the wall of the main graveyard. Bu Qasem didn't forget about me. He'd visit me every night in my dreams. Every time he visited I would ask him the same question. 'Why do you look so sad?' He would answer, 'Because I'm buried in a cold place in the middle of nowhere.' 'What can I do?' 'If only you could dig up my remains and take me home...My final wish is that I be buried under the Hilawi date tree inside our courtyard.'" Her gaze trailed into the distance. "He visited me in my dreams yesterday night. 'After you're done burying me, you must recite the noble Qur'an over my grave for two hours a day for a period of forty days.'"

The message implicit in her last words, the officer motioned her to silence.

"Where are your husband's remains now?" he asked.

"They're sitting inside their shroud at the house."

He came to a decision.

"We'll help you carry out the burial rites today and we'll figure out how to get you out of the no-go areas as soon as that's over."

The anguish sweeping over her made the words hard to process.

"Why 'no-go'?"

"Civilians are prohibited from entering them out of regard for their safety."

She was a woman who'd lived to be a grandmother, she began, her life wasn't any more valuable than the life of young men in the prime of—

"War is war, and nobody thinks with this logic," he stopped her. He continued, "The orders are clear and do not allow esoteric interpretations."

She wished she could tell him openly, *"I don't understand what you mean by esoteric interpretations."*

"What about my husband's final wishes for the recitation of the noble Qur'an?" she asked.

He didn't want to sound harsh. "You and your husband and your final wishes—these are matters for the two of you."

"I don't understand," she said bitterly.

He shook his head. "There's nothing we can do."

She struggled not to let her distress show. "Would you allow me to go back, taking my husband's remains with me?"

He was able to contain his rising impatience at the way she was prolonging the debate. "This is a matter for you to decide."

She could no longer restrain herself. She burst into

56

uncontrollable sobs. He waited for a moment hoping it would stop, but she continued weeping.

"Lady…"

Her wailing continued unabated. A sense of dismay came over him. He had no desire to be fanning the flames of this woman's unhappiness.

"We have strict operational rules that we can't violate. If we did, we'd all be liable to disciplinary action." He was silent for a few seconds. "And that includes you."

Soon she calmed down a little and regained her composure.

"What day of the month is it today?" she asked.

He had no choice but to answer. "The eleventh."

Her voice melted into a plea. "I know my request will be difficult—" she halted mid-sentence.

"First we need to know the request," he prompted her.

"That you allow me to stay in my house until the twenty-first."

"You have the day of Nowruz in mind."

She didn't say, *"It's because I was born on the day of Nowruz."* Shielding her eyes with her hand to hide the tears, she instead said, "Bu Qasem and I were married on the day of Nowruz."

He tried not to let his sense of sympathy show. "You'd like to stay for ten days."

"May God number this among your good deeds," she said ardently.

He meditated silently for a moment. Then he said, troubled, "Every now and then we're subjected to disciplinary inspection."

She thought it best to hold her tongue until he was finished.

57

"What will we tell the authorities if they find out you're here?"

She didn't need to think long.

"You could tell them it's just some silly old lady who's lost her head."

He had to check his laughter. "We'll have to think of an appropriate explanation." She listened carefully as he added more severely, "On condition that you're gone on the morning of the twenty-first."

"The morning of the twenty-first," she shot back hopefully.

He conceded with a nod. "Very well." He continued, "In this case you'll have plenty of time to recite the noble Qur'an over your husband's grave."

A little cry of pleasure escaped her. She rose to her feet. "You're a kind man."

She hurried away, Good Omen following close behind. Now she could let herself relax a little. She had passed the greatest test. The biggest credit went to her body, which had thrown her a lifeline at a strategic moment. Passing out isn't something you can do at will. She had to admit she'd felt a violent shock the moment she'd seen the muzzles of their machine guns pointed at her. She had no choice but to faint. It hadn't been a state of total oblivion to what was going on around her, more a transparent kind of awareness, like being frozen in midair. She could hear them talking back and forth, sounding all worried and confused. They'd never had to deal with a situation like this before. Most of them were young, some of them barely twenty. She was sorry she had to cause them worry, but she needed to stick to her fainting spell if she wanted to achieve her aim of being allowed to stay. She had to admit it was only a partial success, limited to a period of only ten days. Yet there was still a chance she would find some reason or excuse that would convince them to let her stay before this time was up.

The cup of tea, the mouth-watering bread, the lentil soup…then she remembered her donkey. He also needed to eat. As they walked along, the mud wall of the Daleeshiya orchard came up on their left. She drew Good Omen's attention to a spot where there was a gap in the wall. "You'll be able to find something to eat through there."

Good Omen eagerly accepted her suggestion. With a muffled snore, he quickly disappeared into the orchard.

A LITTLE AFTER SHE'D FINISHED smoothing out the floor of the grave, she heard the sound of Good Omen's snorts. She looked up and saw him poking his head over the grave, his way of letting her know he was back. "I'll call you if I need you." He retreated from her line of vision. She lifted her eyes to the sky. White clouds like tufts of cotton wool were almost hiding the sphere of the sun from view. It was the time of the midday heat. There was no reason she needed to rush the burial of Bu Qasem's remains.

Her aim was to make his grave a place that would keep his bones safe and treat them kindly. She remembered their neighbor Mulla Hussein used to keep some building bricks in his house. She knew the bricks were still there, but she didn't know where Mulla Hussein had settled after the evacuation. Should she see him one day she would tell him, *"I had to use a few of your bricks for Bu Qasem's grave."* She was confident she could predict his reply. *"With my blessing, Um Qasem."* She climbed out of the pit. Good Omen noticed and came over. She strapped the saddlebags to his back. "Follow me."

She began by paving the floor of the grave with bricks before buttressing the flanks. It was now beginning to look like a narrow stone casket open at the top. She went and got the cloth with the bones. "In the name of God, the compassionate, the merciful." She set the shroud down inside. "Don't worry, I won't leave your remains out in the open to be eaten away by the soil the way it was in Nasiriya." She brought over a few more bricks and lay them down alongside so as to make a kind of cover for the casket. She cast an appraising last glance over her work. "You're all safe now."

She didn't pour the soil over the grave right away. Instead she headed to her room. The conjugal bed looked just as it had when she had left it on the dawn of the evacuation. The ornamental wooden trunk stood in one corner of the room. She crouched down before it. The thirty parts of the Qur'an lay inside the trunk folded in a white cotton sleeve. She hugged the sleeve to her chest. She decided in favor of the first part, the one that contained the shorter verses. She knew the "Verses of Refuge" by heart, but she wanted to carry out the recitation according to the conventions usually followed in mourning ceremonies.

She was deep into reading when Good Omen emitted a snore that drew her attention. As she turned toward him, she heard the sound of knocking on the door. "It must be the soldiers," she concluded.

"The door is open," she called out.

A soldier stepped inside. He gave a greeting before delivering his message.

"My commanding officer Lieutenant Abdel Kareem sent me."

She noticed he was holding a paper bag. Inside there was some tea and sugar. She accepted the bag from him.

"You're a good bunch."

A look of curiosity appeared in his eyes. "How did you get

here, lady—I heard you came from Najaf."

"I'd like you to use my name—Um Qasem."

"I'm Second Lieutenant Sadeq."

"Give my thanks to your commanding officer. I'm a tea drinker." She went on, "If you have a bit of time I can make some tea for us to drink together. I need to figure out how I should go about things."

He accepted with a smile. "I have all the time in the world."

She looked at him quizzically.

"We're going through a quiet time just now," he explained. "The Iranians take the Nowruz festival very seriously and stop fighting two weeks before the date."

So that's why I didn't see any signs of the war along the way, Um Qasem thought to herself.

She fetched a mat and rolled it out on the ground not far from the grave.

"I can help you bury your departed husband if you wish," he offered.

"Perhaps you can help me figure out how to stay," she said with supplication in her voice.

He didn't try to hide his sense of bafflement. "How?"

She didn't try to hide her bafflement either. "I don't know."

As they drank their tea, she told him about the time she'd spent in Najaf. The sense of grief and longing she'd felt until she finally took the decision to return. Good Omen had held nothing back. Arriving, she'd been shocked at the conditions she'd found. Before the evacuation Sabiliyat had pulsed with life, it was able to survive off its own resources.

"The shrine of Sayyid Rajab Al-Rifaee who's known for his miracles, we used to see dozens of cars drive up to it filled

62

with people coming from far away who'd made pledges…
In those days Sabiliyat was bursting with life." Sorrow over-
whelmed her. "Now it's not only empty of people but life has
gone out of the orchards as well."

Second Lieutenant Sadeq told her he had been one of the
first military personnel to arrive at the scene. Together with the
previous commander of the platoon, he'd taken on the task of
laying out the defense positions, based on guidelines issued by
the division's command. He didn't deny it, the place had been
bursting with green. Military orders had arrived demanding
that they block up the entrances of all rivers leading out of
the Shatt. Things began to wither, and it wasn't long before
everything went barren.

She made no secret of the displeasure she felt. "Why
deprive the orchards of water?"

"Defensive procedures."

Her eyebrows rose in amazement. "Defending against
what?"

He was at a loss how to respond. Could he say, *"They
were blocked up in order to stop Iranian divers from infiltrating our
backlines"?* Were he to elaborate, he could talk to her about
military plans and necessary procedures. The real war was happening elsewhere, as everyone knew, at lines of contact with
the enemy. He knew something about the operations of at-
tack-and-retreat taking place in the border area of Shalamcheh
to the northeast of Basra, or around the saltworks south of
Al-Faw. There was information he wasn't authorized to share
concerning his platoon, which formed part of the regiment
of the armored infantry. Their instructions were to remain
stationed opposite the west coast of the Shatt al-Arab in view

of its vital importance as part of the second line of defense extending from the area of Al-Khoura to Bab Sulayman south of the district of Abul Khaseeb.

He hesitated whether to let her in on what he knew. Yet, here was this woman who had abruptly showed up at their doorstep coming from the precincts of noble Najaf. That she should have crossed hundreds of kilometers with her donkey when the country was crawling with soldiers without running into a single one...that was something that verged on the miraculous. The two of them sitting alone before a pot of tea... He made up his mind to speak freely.

"The war is decided by those higher up the ladder. There's nothing soldiers like us can do except obey blindly."

She didn't try to conceal her astonishment.

"Why blindly?"

"It's just a figure of speech. It means you must obey the orders that come to you without asking questions."

She made a gesture of acceptance, without conviction.

"When we were first deployed, before the war reached its current pitch, there were forty of us here. We put up our tents a short distance from the mansion of the Naqeebs. Even though we took all necessary precautions, from time to time we'd still suffer direct hits from Iranian shells that made it across the border." An involuntary sigh escaped him. "Whenever our numbers would drop, they'd send in fresh recruits to balance them out. We had another commanding officer who was killed inside his Jeep."

She asked him painfully, "How are they able to target you from so far away?"

He seized the opportunity to make a point. "This is why

we have strict orders prohibiting civilians from entering zones of active hostilities."

"God is our keeper."

Concerning the possibility of her staying on indefinitely he said, "The only person who can grant that kind of request is Lieutenant Abdel Kareem."

"He's a kind-hearted young man," she said. "He gave me permission to stay for ten days." There was ardor in her voice. "If we could only convince him to extend this time…" She trailed off.

He felt it was best to be straight. "I don't believe he has the authority to allow you to stay for an unlimited duration."

"I don't want to stay for an unlimited duration. A few weeks would be enough."

"Were a disciplinary committee to come by, or a high-ranking officer to show up, Lieutenant Abdel Kareem would face questioning."

"Would they hold him to account for the fact that I'm here?" she asked with surprise.

"The first question they'd ask him would be, 'How did this woman get here?'"

Playing along, she imagined herself into his shoes. "He'd say, 'I've no idea who she is. She just turned up here one day out of the blue.'"

Second Lieutenant Sadeq gave a wry little laugh. "There's no room for these kinds of replies in military inquests."

"You're making things sound harder than they are," she complained.

"I'm just being honest."

She couldn't find anything to say in reply…

"Nobody wants to live in a danger zone. Why are you so keen to stay?"

"The request of my husband Bu Qasem."

Her answer took him aback. "Did he give instructions in his will?"

"Not his will."

He fixed his eyes on her, waiting for her to clarify.

"He visits me in my dreams every other night and asks me to stay by his side."

He made no effort to hide his astonishment. "It would be better if he tried to make sure you stay alive by leaving a military zone."

"This isn't only about Bu Qasem. I can't go on living away from here."

He pondered her words. His next question followed a different drift. "You have children."

Her voice became radiant with love. "I have sons and daughters and grandchildren."

"Where are they?"

"In Najaf."

"How can you live apart from them?"

"They're busy with their own lives." She ran her eyes over the doors of the rooms in her house. "Someone has to be here to keep things going. Empty houses fall to ruin." He had already settled on a response when she continued, "Who will relieve Bu Qasem's loneliness?"

"I don't understand the way you think," he told her plainly. "I'd give half my life just to have a single day with my family."

"Where are they?"

"In Mosul."

"Mosul is a long way away," she remarked. "When did you last visit them?"

"I haven't visited them once."

"Aren't soldiers entitled to leave?"

"When the circumstances of war allow." She didn't catch his meaning. Not a month went by without someone getting injured, occasionally killed. Again she didn't catch his meaning. How could someone who's just finished picking up what's left of his comrade find the heart to ask for furlough? A look of pained understanding appeared in her eyes. She didn't imagine they buried the fallen right there? A military ambulance would come around to collect the bodies. She felt an urge to ask him how many had been killed, but she thought better of it. Instead, she asked when would this war of theirs come to an end?

"Nobody knows for sure," he said with a helpless air.

If only she could ask what good the war was serving. He'd likely respond, *"Soldiers are not to ask questions."*

While they were busy talking, Good Omen drew up to the basin connected to the tap in the middle of the courtyard, where there were still a few traces of water. He brought his snout to it and began lapping up the water noisily.

"Even though the war is going on, there's water still coming from the tap," Um Qasem observed.

"The first few months we were here there was no running water. They'd meet our needs by bringing water tankers around. Then the engineering wing of the army managed to get the water treatment plant at the outskirts of Abul Khaseeb back up and running." He smiled before continuing. "Once, this plant was subjected to direct shelling from the Iranian side and the water was cut for two whole weeks."

"Same story as the water of the Shatt," she concluded.

After he was gone, she approached the pit of her husband's grave. "I don't imagine you're in a special hurry for me to pack the soil." She continued apologetically, "I'll need to leave you on your own for a little while." She turned to Good Omen. "Let's take a walk through the village."

To see things in passing or by chance is one thing; to specifically set out to see them is another. During the evacuation it hadn't occurred to her to cast a lingering glance over the particulars of the place so as to fix their images in her memory. At the time she had been wholly engrossed by the shock of the parting. During the time she'd spent living in the shack next to the graveyard in Najaf, she'd struggled with all her might to recall specific details of her life here, but all she'd managed to glean were emotional impressions left behind by moments she'd lived during that bygone time. If she had to struggle so hard, it was only because that time was no longer. All that was left of Sabiliyat was a patchwork of blurred forms that she was unable to bring to life. Now she could get her relationship to her surroundings on a firm footing.

She didn't take the trouble to lock up behind her. Apart from the soldiers on the Shatt, there were no signs of life anywhere in the area. She looked meditatively all around. To her right stood the house of Deaf Abboud. He was a carpenter who specialized in closets and beds. Young people planning to get married would always make him their port of call. She remembered one time she'd asked for his help to repair the frame of the bed she shared with Bu Qasem. He had refused to take payment for his work. His refusal had taken her aback. "But why, Abboud?" "I made this bed and it's my job to maintain it," he had replied with quiet satisfaction.

She remembers the way she used to communicate with him using hand gestures. He had acquired his nickname, Deaf Abboud, after he'd lost his hearing. His carpentry workshop doubled as his house. His sister Hameeda was the one who managed the household, even though she was also deaf. The house was made up of a small room with two beds and a larger room that served as a carpentry workshop. She knew that Abboud and Hameeda didn't lock their door with a bolt. Deaf people can't hear you knock, so visitors would have to let themselves in and then they'd come into the sight of Abboud, who spent all his mornings in his workshop.

Is there any reason not to? Um Qasem thought to herself. She gave a push to the door. The hallway came into view. She turned to Good Omen and said to him, "You're free to go in." He was pleased by her proposal. He welcomed it with a toss of his head. He crossed the hallway and then made a beeline for the carpentry room. *Maybe it's the smell of sawdust,* the thought came to her. She hung back for a few seconds. Absence had its own distinctive music. Her imagination drifted, reviving the echo of Abboud's saw as it buzzed steadily along or the sound of his hammer falling. She took a few steps into the courtyard. Her eyes wandered to the plum tree. She felt her heart sink. The plum tree was struggling to stay alive. Most of its leaves had died from lack of water. The ground of the courtyard was carpeted with its shriveled leaves. She noticed a few low-lying branches that were still streaked with green and had a few clusters of small fruit on them.

When Hameeda was still around she used to dote on this

tree, which would shower her with fruit every season without fail. She'd make sure she cut down the clusters before they were ripe and then add them to the pickle mix, which was normally made of cucumbers, tomatoes, turnip, carrots, aubergines, and garlic. Their distinctive aroma and unique taste made the plums stand out in this mix. Um Qasem remembers what her daughter Hasna had said one evening after she'd paid for a ceramic jar of mixed pickles. "What Hameeda makes selling pickles is almost more than what her brother Abboud makes from his carpentry work." She remembers the reply her son Saleh had made. "It's because she's deaf as a doorknob that she's got the pickle market wrapped in her palm," he'd quipped. She can almost hear her husband's reprimand. "You shouldn't make other people's handicaps the butt of your jokes."

How could memories feel so breathtakingly real? A sense of emptiness yawned inside her chest. No one could say with confidence when the war would end and life would return to normal, and she wasn't confident she'd be able to stay away from them indefinitely. Good Omen emerged from the carpentry room, his jaws working away on something. He then headed for the arbor at the far end of the courtyard where the pickle jars were kept. Her gaze drifting in that direction, she saw a number of ceramic jars standing there in rows. Good Omen brought his snout to them, had a sniff, and then tossed his head disapprovingly. Had he picked up on the pungent smell of vinegar?

She approached the jars. There were a good few of them. Though they seemed to be shut tight, there were still traces of vinegar in the air. Crouching down in front of one of the jars, she rocked it from side to side and she discovered it was full.

70

When they'd received the evacuation order, Hameeda must have figured they'd be back in three months. No reason why they shouldn't leave the pickles there until…Hameeda hadn't come back, and in the meantime the pickles had matured and developed an even richer aroma. She examined some of the other jars and discovered they were all full to the brim. Since the master of the house was absent, Um Qasem would be doing nothing wrong if she helped herself to some of these pickles. It was only proper she should repay Lieutenant Abdel Kareem for the generosity he'd shown sending her the tea and sugar. If Hameeda returned one day, Um Qasem would lose no time paying her back for what she'd taken.

Her thoughts turned to the suffering plum tree. The water basin connected to the tap that stood in the middle of the courtyard was only a short distance from the trunk of the tree. She twisted the knob and there was a hiss before water came spurting out. Good Omen cantered over to have a drink. Um Qasem gave a smile of satisfaction. Using a carpenter's axe that belonged to the owner of the house, she steered the water toward the plum tree. She strained to listen. There was a sound like whispering in the first few moments as the parched earth began to soak up the water. She gazed at the branches of the plum tree. She had the sense it was communicating its joy. Trees have their own special language. "I won't neglect to water you," Um Qasem pledged.

- 6 -

TROTTING ALONG AHEAD OF HER, Good Omen headed for the gap in the wall of the Daleeshiya orchard. Smiling at his initiative, she followed him in. She breathed in the air of the orchard. Why this smell of dry stalks everywhere, mixed with an acrid stench like that of something fermenting? It seemed that plants had their own way of declaring the fact that they were surrendering to death. The wan yellow of the palm leaves, the two mulberry trees facing their death sentence standing upright, their branches bare and a wreath of dry leaves around their trunks. Thirty whole months without water. Who was it that had killed them? Trying to analyze the causes and effects only made one sad.

She saw Good Omen weaving his way through the empty creeks looking for any grasses that might still be growing there. Oh, to let her eyes drift through the orchard…Before the evacuation, the foliage used to be so dense you could hardly see where you were going. There were pomegranate trees and grapevines, besides apricot, orange, and tangerine trees. She remembers how this orchard used to run all the way to Sayyid Rajab River where the banana trees stood, at the point where the bank began to slope toward the water, their oversized leaves a lustrous green. She was surprised to find her heart had begun

72

to thump. Before she knew it, her memory was surging with images from the past. The way the river used to flow at high tide, that special color it had, which was a cross between the green of leaves and the blue of the sky. She remembers how it would rush up against the banks in large billowing waves.

She noticed that Good Omen had disappeared from sight. "Good Omen!" she called out. She heard his snore and then she saw him stick out his neck to indicate his location. He was standing inside one of the dry creeks at one end of the rear wall of Mahmoud Abbas's house. What had drawn him there? She quickly made her way over. Dry leaves kept snapping under her feet. She saw the branches of the Bambawi Christ's-thorn tree that stood inside Mahmoud Abbas's house dangling over the wall, looking all yellow. As she drew nearer, she noticed that Good Omen was munching at some of the nabk fruit that had fallen into the creek. She could hardly believe her eyes. This was the first time in her life she was seeing a donkey eating nabk. Was he so hungry or was it the sheer abundance? She knew her Good Omen well. If the fruit had been rotten he would never have come near it.

She took a few steps farther. The ground right behind the wall of Mahmoud Abbas's house was blanketed with the same fruit. Some of it was dry and looked like it had fallen a long time ago, while some of it looked relatively fresh. A thrill of excitement ran through her. She remembered this was the only tree in Sabiliyat that yielded good quality nabk of the Bambawi sort, with its large oval shape, its tawny skin, and its taste like that of a lightly fermented apple. Her mouth had begun to water. She didn't try to resist. She bent down, picked out a fruit, wiped it off with the hem of her dress, and then popped it into her mouth. It tasted exactly as she remembered it.

She looked up at the branches overhanging the wall. The purple hue of the leaves spoke of severe thirst. She knew that Christ's-thorn trees, like date palms, had the capacity to endure thirst, but water was of vital importance. Her mind drifted, taking her back to the time before the war with all its everyday detail. Mahmoud Abbas had owned the only grocery store in Sabiliyat, where people would go to buy their food essentials. He'd then sold it to Blind Khudayr and relocated his business to the Al-Maqam souk in the district of Al-Ashar. Her mind quickened, bringing back pictures from the courtyard that lay behind the wall. The refined taste of that fellow Mahmoud Abbas...the ornate doors of the rooms and the windows that gave on to the courtyard, the damask rose shrubs planted in a circle around the trunk of the Christ's-thorn tree. The water fountain standing in the corner, the way the damask roses would bloom always soaking in its water.

Her ears strained to pick up any sign of life coming from behind the wall. For a moment she had the impression she could hear a nightingale warbling. In the old days they used to keep a nightingale inside a hanging cage fashioned out of palm tree branches. The nightingale's sense of confinement compared with the freedom enjoyed by the dozens of birds nesting inside the Christ's-thorn tree, the plaintive song the captive would make and the way the uncaged birds would answer... She recoiled a little. There was no nightingale warbling.

What if she were to—? She halted mid-thought, the decision already taken. *I'll pop my head over the wall for starters.* She walked up to the corner of the wall. There was an elevation

74

in the ground there that made it possible to look down into the courtyard. She saw the dry leaves of the Christ's-thorn tree covering the courtyard like a mottled carpet. The doors and windows of the rooms were all tightly sealed. Mahmoud Abbas's family had thought they would be coming back in three months' time. The damask rose shrubs had turned into dry stalks.

She could no longer stay put. She turned toward Good Omen. "Come here." He drew up to her compliantly. "Stand still and don't move." He was quick to obey. She climbed onto his back and stood up with her feet planted on his shoulders. She was now in a position to scale the wall without much trouble. "I'll only be a few minutes," she said to Good Omen reassuringly. She was careful making her way down into the courtyard. She wouldn't face the same difficulty when she decided to leave, she'd be able to open the front door from the inside.

She cast a searching look around. There was a tap standing right beside the bed of the Christ's-thorn tree. She went up to the knob. The water spurted out followed by its usual hiss. Her attention was suddenly drawn to an odd-looking gash running across the wall of the kitchen. Where had that gash come from? She drew nearer. Curiosity spurring her, she poked her head through the opening. She saw pieces of shattered brick lying all over the kitchen floor. Her mind began to work. It must have been one of them who caused this damage. She reached for the door handle and it responded. The darkness dissipated. She found herself staring down at a gaping hole in the kitchen floor. Something that looked like an iron funnel was jutting out of the hole. She felt her mouth going dry. The effects of their war. She stepped back with caution. Her mind was unable to fathom how this incongruous thing could have gotten there.

She rushed toward the front door. She slid the iron bolt open and was surprised to find Good Omen standing right in front of her. She was even more surprised to see Second Lieutenant Sadeq standing just a few steps away. Good Omen gave a welcoming nod, and Second Lieutenant Sadeq said, "Lieutenant Abdel Kareem ordered me to look for you." She was about to ask, *"Anything wrong?"* but he continued, "I went to your house but no one was there. On my way back I spotted your donkey standing here."

She felt an urge to comment on Good Omen's good sense, but then she remembered what had made her anxious and decided to seek the benefit of her companion's experience.

"Come here just a minute."

Leading the way in, she brought him to the kitchen door.

"What is this?" She pointed to the iron funnel sticking out of the hole in the floor.

"A cannon shell."

She didn't try to disguise her sense of alarm. "Is it dangerous?"

His lips parted in a reassuring smile. "Once it's exploded and served its purpose, it's as good as scrap metal."

She watched closely as he approached the object and bent over it. He reached out and rotated it in place with one hand until he had dislodged it from the hole. She noticed the iron was splintered at the head.

"How did their shell get here all this way?"

"It came from their artillery bases behind the lines of contact."

It didn't occur to her to ask what he meant by lines of contact.

"You'll find dozens of shells lying around after they've fallen on houses or in the orchards."

"They take aim at houses and fire at date palms," she muttered with irritation.

"There have been times when our tents suffered direct hits." Sadness washed into his voice. "Some of our men lost their lives."

"When will they be done with this war?" she asked, sharing his emotion.

"Nobody knows…"

She stared at him in surprise.

"…whenever it pleases them."

There was no longer any reason for her to linger. She headed toward the door, Second Lieutenant Sadeq following close behind.

"What does Lieutenant Abdel Kareem want?"

"He wants to make sure you've had lunch."

A feeling of gratitude flooded into her.

"God bless him… What time is it?"

"Half past three."

She motioned toward the mosque's minaret in the distance.

"In the past, the call to prayer would tell us the time."

How would the other interpret her remark?

"I'll be with you shortly," she added.

She made sure the pickle jar was securely hitched to Good Omen's saddle. "It's by way of a gift," she said to her donkey matter-of-factly.

They left the house of Deaf Abboud and began following the road toward the part of the Shatt where the soldiers were based. That morning when they'd carried her to their camp she'd been in such a daze she hadn't had a chance to take in the surroundings in proper detail. Her mind had been working along a single track, how to ensure she could stay here. "What do you think?" she asked Good Omen. Good Omen made a sound like a muffled sneeze. "I promise to take you to the Shatt so can you drink from it."

Cool gusts of wind brushed against her face, traveling down the road from the east. The old building that served as a stable for Sayyid Taleb Basha Al-Naqeeb's horses stood to the right, the houses of his servants and attendants to the left. She caught sight of a hole at the topside of one of the walls that formed part of the stable. What was the sense in their firing their shells this way? As she came up alongside the gate of the mansion, she saw it was bolted and covered in dust.

The sound of men muttering among themselves reached her ears. She caught glimpse of a number of small camouflaged tents standing inside the orchard that gave onto the Shatt. The Shatt lay before her, stretching out as far as the eye could see. She felt a sudden impulse to break into a run. Lieutenant Abdel Kareem's voice claimed her attention. There was surprise in it.

"What is it you've brought on your donkey?" He was standing at the entrance of his tent.

"A little treat for you," she replied.

He didn't get her meaning.

"A jar of pickles."

"Soldiers don't eat pickles," he objected.

"Why not?" she asked in amazement.

For a couple of seconds he was at a loss how to reply.

"Because pickles are a luxury."

She didn't try to argue with him further. Instead she proceeded to unhitch the container from Good Omen's back, and the donkey dashed off toward the Shatt. Um Qasem reached for the lid and twisted it. The mouth-watering aroma of the pickles wafted through the air.

"The premium sort," Lieutenant Abdel Kareem conceded.

"It'll go perfectly with a plate of grilled fish."

"We don't eat grilled fish," he said regretfully.

She gestured toward the Shatt. "It's all out there waiting."

"We have to adhere to the regulations."

"Why?"

He laughed. "You have a right to ask questions, but we have a duty to follow the instructions laid down by our superiors."

Holding her last "why" back, she screwed the lid back onto the container, unable to conceal her sense of disappointment.

"Since you don't want it…"

He gave another laugh. "But we won't refuse it."

She studied him as he went on.

"Because it's a gift from you."

A look of joy swept over her face. "Thank you."

He didn't try to hide his curiosity. He pointed toward the spot right by the Shatt where Good Omen had come to a halt. "What's your donkey doing?"

"I promised him a drink at the Shatt."

He was overcome by astonishment. "You promised your donkey."

She took her time eating the meal they put before her. She noticed there was too much salt in the food but she didn't say anything to them. She turned to Lieutenant Abdel Kareem.

"Perhaps you could give me and Good Omen permission to have a walk around the Shatt?"

"Since this is a time of truce, there's no objection," he replied.

The idea that she might be targeted by some mysterious enemy was so foreign to her mind she could hardly take it seriously. Good Omen quickly trotted over and caught up with her. She made her way along the embankment, following the Shatt all the way from the mud dam standing at the mouth of Sayyid Rajab River down to the second dam at the mouth of Chouma River. It pained her to see the Shatt surging with water and pulsing with life while these rivers were reduced to deep muddy trenches overgrown with reeds and papyrus plants. What gave them the right to sentence the orchards to death?

When they had gone some distance from the army camp, Good Omen came to a stubborn halt. She understood what he was proposing, she knew him well. He was asking her to mount him. "Since you insist," she said to him affectionately. She was surprised to find him leading her to the half-open door of Mahmoud Abbas's house. "It's as if you were doing my thinking for me," she laughed. The image of the water pouring out of the tap suddenly flashed before her. A sense of anxiety came over her. The water overflowing in the courtyard. She dismounted. "You can go in." She rushed to the tap and turned it off. The bed of the tree had overflowed and the courtyard was covered in a sheet of water. She saw Good Omen dip his snout into the shallow water, pluck out the nabk fruit, and chew at them unhurriedly. She looked up at the Christ's-thorn tree. "You'll have to be patient until your branches turn green."

She turned her eyes toward the wall of the kitchen. This ugly hole, disfiguring the whole place. Since there was no one else in Sabiliyat besides her, she had to face up to her responsibilities. The decision welled up in her. This splintered piece of iron they'd put here can't be allowed to stay. She headed for the kitchen, Good Omen on her heels. She stopped short before the piece of iron. "Help me carry it outside the house," she said to Good Omen. She lifted up the piece of iron and hoisted it over Good Omen's saddlebag. He led the way out of the house and she followed close behind.

She hadn't had a specific place in mind to take the piece of iron and dispose of it, so how could Good Omen have one? He kept walking along a few meters ahead of her. He passed her house and continued his course in the direction of Abul Khaseeb Road. It occurred to her that perhaps he was taking her to Ezz el-Deen Cemetery. Her prediction was disproven when he veered to the right, turning into a vacant piece of land where leftover building materials lay about in heaps next to a number of oversized cement pipes that had gone unused because of the war. "Good choice," she commented appreciatively. She steered him toward the pit where the rubbish was dumped and she tipped the piece of iron into it.

Back at the house, she crouched down before the open top of her husband's grave. She fixed her eyes on the brick lining inside. "Since you're listening…" she began. "Sabiliyat right now, dozens of soldiers everywhere…I know you're not troubled by what's happening all around you. As far as Good Omen and I are concerned, we've nothing to fear from their war. Everyone dies when their time comes. What I'm really afraid of is when the ten days are up and it's time to be turned out." She thought intently for a few moments. "I promise I won't give you up."

Her first night in their shared bed, reliving the details of the last night she'd spent in the house before the evacuation. Everyone anxious, confused, asking questions that had no answers. What would it be like, the day that was dawning, where to, for how long. None of her family had found the time to go to bed. She recalls the question she'd put to her husband. "Who will look after our house while we're away?" She remembers how he'd turned aside so she wouldn't notice the tears in his eyes. "There's no reason we need to hide our sorrow, Bu Qasem," she'd felt like pleading. She strained her ears to listen to the darkness around. There wasn't a trace of any of the familiar nighttime noises. Life in all its variety depended on that one fundamental element, water.

She couldn't say for sure when she nodded off. Lucidity came to her out of the depths of featureless time. She grew suddenly alert to discover Bu Qasem had resolved to go out of the house. "Why do you want to go out in the pitch of night?" "It's safer in the dark," he replied. "It's no longer safe, the place is crawling with soldiers," she protested. She had the sense he wanted to pacify her. "The soldiers aren't interested in monitoring what goes on outside their tents." She noticed he was holding an axe in his hands. She looked more closely. It was none other than Deaf Abboud's.

"Why the axe?" she asked in some surprise. "Somebody has to do what's necessary." *Now he's started speaking in riddles,* she thought to her herself. Did he divine what was turning in her thoughts? "They're not riddles, Um Qasem." He went on, "Those mud barriers they've put at the entrances of our rivers—" He didn't finish his sentence. "These mud barriers are no trifling matter," she shot back. His response took her aback.

"At midnight the tide reaches its peak on the Shatt and comes up almost to the top of the dam. If we dig a small furrow along the top, the water will weigh up its forces and push its way into the interior." She was speechless with amazement. "You talk about the water as if it was a living thing." His response was trenchant. "So it is." Somewhere as she was oscillating between belief and disbelief, he must have slipped out the door.

Sensation returned to her limbs. She opened her eyes. She had fallen asleep on their shared bed. The night and its deafening silence. The realization came back, Bu Qasem is dead. "In the name of God, the compassionate, the merciful," she murmured. Her heart flew out to her husband. She sat up. Why the axe? She was gripped by a sudden desire to go to his grave. She quickly stepped outside. She stood facing the pit and began reciting the short verses she knew by heart.

HER THOUGHTS GREW QUIETER after she had recited the two "Verses of Refuge." She gazed deep into the grave. "What is it you're trying to tell me?" She wasn't expecting a reply. She tried to go over in her mind some of the things that had happened since her arrival. It was hard for her to process the fact that she had only been there since yesterday. The fronds of the Hilawi date palm stirred, responding to the gusts of a passing wind. She drew the hem of her dress tightly around herself. There was a pinch in the air. The light of dawn was slowly beginning to spread. She heard Good Omen utter a snore, letting her know he was inside the pen. The question of how to make sure he had food no longer weighed on her mind. "Good Omen!" He stepped out of the pen and stood there with an expectant air. "You can go to the Daleeshiya," she said.

When there's nothing to keep your mind busy, your bodily needs begin to clamor for attention. She felt a sharp pang in her stomach. She needed to find a way to allay her hunger. She couldn't leave the issue of getting food to luck. Why not have a look around the pantry? She hurried over. The stove that had sat deserted ever since the evacuation day, the shelf where they kept the canned food. A bit of salt, some spices, the ceramic jar where the rice was stored. A little rice was better than none. She spread out a rag over the ground of the courtyard and tipped out the grains of rice onto it. She had to make sure it was safe to cook, clearing out those tiny insects that looked like lice. Another jar contained a dollop of lentils, that one had its share of insects too. Cleaning out the grains meant baring them to the sun.

She felt a sudden sense of deflation. The amount of grains remaining was small, it would only last her a couple of days. What about the days after that? It wouldn't do for her to be relying on handouts from the soldiers. Her mind began to rummage through the possibilities. Experience told her that there had to be cooking supplies laid up in the houses of the well-to-do. Since she was the only one in the village, she had a right to appropriate whatever food might be available. She remembered the kitchen in Mahmoud Abbas's house. When she had gone there the previous day, she hadn't paid any attention to the containers lined up along the walls, and she hadn't given a look to the door of the dry goods storeroom that was near the kitchen.

An hour later, Good Omen came back. "Let's go to Mahmoud Abbas's." Her eyes drifted up and down the road. There was no sign of life at this morning hour. In the time before, Sabiliyat would have been bursting with life. She walked past the gate of the boys' school. The thought took root, it wouldn't be right for the children to come back and find everything destroyed from the impact of shells crossing through. *I'll find a moment to have a look around the school from the inside.* As soon as they were through the door of the house, Good Omen set about looking for nabk fruits. She picked up a fruit in her turn, wiped it clean with her dress, and raised it to her mouth. This taste that was unlike all others. Her sense of hunger intensified.

Going into the kitchen, she saw a number of large ceramic containers stacked alongside each other. She lifted the
lid off the first. There was enough rice inside to keep her
going for months. She felt a sense of pressure in her chest.
There was no guarantee she'd still be here after the day of
Nowruz. She put the lid back in place. The only thing she
needed to do now was clear out the insects. She moved on to
the next container. It was filled with wheat flour. She cast a
searching glance around her. She caught sight of an iron sheet
that was used for making bread. The whole affair wouldn't
take her more than an hour.

As she was chewing on the warm sugar pastry, her eyes
fell on the broken bricks scattered over the kitchen floor.
She'd gotten rid of the piece of splintered iron yesterday, but
the splintered wall was still there. Her jaw suddenly stopped
moving. She couldn't be laying hands on things that belonged
to the people of this house without giving something back.
The decision made her mind light up with pleasure. I will
repair the wall of their kitchen. After she had finished eating,
she began to sweep up the scattered bricks. Going up to the
Christ's-thorn tree, she saw that the soil in its bed had grown
spongy from the soaking it had received on the previous day.
She made use of the wet soil to fit the bricks into the hole
in the wall. She stepped back and surveyed the results of her
labor. She had to admit she was no professional builder but
she had done the best she could. Her eyes traveled to the dry
branches of the damask rose shrub. *Where can I find a live shrub
of damask rose so I can bring a few cuttings to plant?*

The idea of clearing the courtyard from the piles of
leaves that had fallen from the Christ's-thorn tree struck her

as appealing. She rolled up the hem of her dress and fell to work. While she was busy working, Good Omen uttered a snort of warning. "What is it?" Her ears picked up the sound of someone knocking on the door. This wasn't her house that she should give permission to anyone, yet the situation being what it was... "It's open!" she called out.

Lieutenant Abdel Kareem stepped through the door, followed by Second Lieutenant Sadeq. The first man broke into a surprised smile. "Why are you tiring yourself out?"

"There's no tiredness." She made a sweeping motion with her hand over the courtyard. "It needs cleaning."

Instead of commenting on her reply he said, "We called by your house to make sure you're alright."

"I haven't cleaned the courtyard of my house yet," she broke in.

"You've left your husband's grave open," he said critically.

"Because I can't guarantee I'll be able to stay by his side." Her response took him aback.

"Will you take his remains with you when you leave?"

"In accordance with his request."

"Does your husband appear to you regularly?"

"Once a night...If your time allows, I can tell you about the visit he paid me early this morning."

He concealed his curiosity behind a smile. "My time allows."

She told him about Bu Qasem arming himself with the carpenter's axe and declaring his plan to knock down the mud dams the soldiers had built at the mouth of the Sayyid Rajab and Chouma Rivers. Lieutenant Abdel Kareem reacted with a sort of bewilderment.

"These mud barriers have been there since before we arrived. It was the army's engineering units that put them up."

"What good do they serve?"

"We follow orders and don't ask questions."

Was it a sense of awkwardness that came over Um Qasem? "I didn't mean…"

Second Lieutenant Sadeq whispered something into the other's ear, pointing to the wall of the kitchen with the freshly repaired segment.

"Why do you go to all this trouble?"

"The sight of the hole was painful on the eyes," she replied.

The first man strode forward, put his head through the kitchen door, and informed his superior, "I think she removed the projectile from where it was."

"Where have you taken it?"

Um Qasem was seized by a sense of unease.

"I didn't know you needed it…I threw it in the dump."

"You're one of a kind," he muttered.

After the two men had left, she finished sweeping the courtyard. She remembered the dry goods storeroom, which she hadn't inspected yet. Her eyes widened with delight as she made out several sacks sitting inside filled with rice, flour, sugar, tea leaves, lentils, mung beans, and other pulses, in addition to metal cans filled with oil, dates, and honeyed dates. With any luck they might not have gone off yet. She picked up a dusty-looking date made with syrup, aniseed, and sesame and popped it into her mouth. There was nothing quite like its pure tang. She stopped short before a can filled with unripe dates that had been boiled and dried. She scooped up a handful and stuffed them into her pocket.

Her imagination began to work away. If this was the harvest from Mahmoud Abbas's storeroom, what might she find in the houses of other well-to-do families? As she was getting ready to leave, her eyes roved across the courtyard. *How can I get hold of some shoots of damask rose?* She fell to thinking. *There are no live plants except at the Shatt where there's water.* She turned to Good Omen and said, "We might be able to find what we're looking for." She added by way of clarification, "We have to pay a visit to Sayyid Rajab's shrine." Her donkey sprung into step and led the way out the door.

Places carried their own meanings, bringing back events from the past and faces of people belonging to a bygone time. The place standing empty of its people, the walls and doors of houses harboring silence, everything invited despair. The whole of life was in a state of forced arrest. She remembers the main street, the side alleys, the people bustling about, the children playing and shouting, the chickens you'd see running about in front of you as you walked along. She strained her ears to listen. Everything deserted and the silence all-encompassing. She was certain it was the absence of water, the network of streams and ponds that had run dry. Living creatures with the power of movement had had no choice but to escape to greener parts. Bu Qasem had indicated to her the means of remedying this barren state. What seemed impenetrable to her was his notion of using the axe of Deaf Abboud. Standing before any of these dams, one could see they reached all the way up to the shoulders of land that flanked them measuring a whole ten meters across, wide enough for their vehicles to pass. What chance did an axe stand against—?

She walked past the door of Jawad Al-Daleeshi's house. The marble arch over the door frame and the five windows giving onto the street made the house stand out from the buildings around it. She had it in mind she might later have a look around Al-Daleeshi's house and also around the garden that made up its backyard. Leading the way, Good Omen turned right into an alley. This is where the taxi driver, Kazem Duck, had his house. He'd gotten his nickname from his fat wife, who was so overweight she would rock sideways when she walked. The nickname also washed off on her son Adel, whom they called Adel Duck. Her daughter Adeela was a model of grace and beauty and she had a nickname all her own, they called her Pretty Adeela.

She came up before the soaring windows of Sayyid Rajab Mosque, with their blue frames that were set off by the white of the plastered walls. This was the only mosque in the area that didn't have a minaret. It was a story that had been passed down from one generation to the next among the villagers. When the eldest Naqeeb had begun building this mosque nearly a hundred years ago, he had taken the decision to raise the entire ceiling and bring it to a level with the minarets of the neighboring village. All he'd done after that was add an architectural flourish that resembled a small turret on each corner of the roof.

Good Omen picked up pace and veered to the left, making his way up the hilly plain where the old graveyard stood with Sayyid Rajab's shrine in the middle. She sped up in turn. She came to a stop before the white building of the shrine. Its high ceiling and large windows made it a kind of miniature copy of the mosque, an overtopping dome lending it added solemnity. To the left of the shrine stood a massive Christ's-thorn tree. She remembers how its branches used to fan out, casting a shadow dozens of meters across that took in the mosque, the shrine, and part of the grounds of the graveyard. She gazed at the tree. Its branches were almost entirely bare. It was said that this tree had been standing there since before the mosque and the shrine were built, which would make it the oldest tree in Basra. She remembers the somewhat tart taste of its nabk fruits. Certain morbid minds used to put about that the reason they were so tart was because they fed off the bones of the dead. Before the war, this Christ's-thorn tree used to provide shelter to countless starlings, nightingales, and pigeons. Their cataclysm of voices would reach even the most distant houses in the village at sunrise or sunset. How could the absence of water—?

The wooden door that gave out to a side path running alongside Sayyid Rajab River was still where she remembered it. She stood there facing the dry trench of the river. On the bank opposite was a piece of farmland that belonged to Sayyid Zayd Al-Naqeeb. This was where he'd hold his customary social gatherings every day in the evening. People called it the Apple Field because of the number of apple trees that grew there in particular profusion. She studied the opposite bank with her eyes. A bitter taste collected under her tongue. Where were the apple trees standing in rows, apricot trees and grape-vine trellises dotted all around them? All she could see was ashen stalks. She cast a look all around her. Dry land was a sign of death. She recoiled a little inside. She shook her head. There was no room for Bu Qasem's scheme and Deaf Abboud's axe.

She approached the eastern entrance of the shrine and followed the four steps down. There were two marble benches on either side, the remains of some mats made out of woven palm leaves, and a paneled wooden door that was covered with henna stains. In the past, this door used to be shut with a bolt fitted with an iron lock. The imam's wife kept the key, and she would only open it when visitors arrived. They would give her a symbolic amount in recognition of her services in looking after the place and keeping it tidy besides handling their gifts. Where had that lock gone? She gave a push to the door and it yielded with a loud creak. Her senses quickened taking in the scent of a light gust that wafted out from within. She should have a look through Mahmoud Abbas's or some of the other houses, maybe she'd be able to locate some incense sticks.

She stepped into the room. The sunshine streaming through the colored glass of the upper windows breathed a deep sense of peace. The rectangular tomb draped in a thick cloth shimmering in different shades of green, the stone benches lined against the walls with straw mats spread over them. The marble shelves jutting out of the walls, the residue of old wax still visible on them. Everything lay under a thick coat of dust. She should make sure she put some time aside for this place.

She heard Good Omen snorting. She looked through the open door and saw him standing outside. "You're free to go wherever you want." Good Omen wandered off. She needed some time alone with herself. She sat down on the floor with her back propped against the tomb. "Oh Sayyid Rajab," she said beseechingly. "When will this war end and the people of Sabiliyat come home?"

- 8 -

SHE'D NEVER EXPERIENCED A NUMBNESS like the one creeping down her neck now. She found herself wondering, how would she manage to break free from it? At that very moment the sound of snorts penetrated into her hearing. Consciousness swept back over her. Of course, it was Good Omen. She opened her eyes. *How did sleep get the better of me like this?* She was sitting inside the tomb of Sayyid Rajab as before. She had no clear sense what time it was.

She saw Good Omen standing outside the door. He'd come back to look for her. Perhaps it was the sense of peace she felt here. She'd slumbered in the shrine of Ezz Al-Din in just the same way. She needed a moment to pull her thoughts together. Those dreams that stole over her out of a timeless present left her mind struggling. That strange dream she'd had right before she woke up, she was at a loss to understand its connections.

She'd dreamt she was twelve and she was wishing she could go to sleep and wake up fourteen years old the next morning. She was fascinated by the expression women often used to describe a beautiful girl. "She's a full moon of fourteen." She asked her mother what the connection was between the moon and the number. "That's when the moon becomes full," her mother answered. The dream went on. She found herself watching her son Saleh as he went about his favorite pastime, fishing. He cast his nets near the entrance of Sayyid Rajab River and bided his time until midnight on the fourteenth day of the Hijri month. "The tide reaches its peak when the moon becomes full," he explained.

She watched him bide his time until the midnight of the twenty-eighth as well. "The tide reaches its peak when the moon disappears completely," he explained. She could understand why her son Saleh would appear in her dream given his passion for fishing, but she was mystified to see her husband appear wielding the axe of Deaf Abboud. "Where are you going?" she confronted him disapprovingly. "I have to give your son Saleh a hand," he replied as he was heading for the door. "He won't be able to catch a single fish if the mud dams stay put," he added. She was at a loss how to understand her dream. Had it been like the previous one, she would have dismissed it as one of those silly dreams that meant nothing. But the fact that it had come to her inside the shrine of Sayyid Rajab...She took the pulse of her thoughts. *If I were to take this seriously, who could help me interpret it?*

She took a slow turn around the shrine and examined all four of its walls carefully. It was a thing to feel proud of: the shells coming from beyond the Shatt had left the walls untouched. There were signs of a shell having landed on an old effaced grave. Another shell had landed a few feet away from the trunk of the Christ's-thorn tree. She turned to look at the wall of the mosque. There was some light damage on the parapet that ran along the roof. The sight was painful on the eyes.

She turned into the passageway that led to a pool of water serving the visitors of the shrine. She remembers a story the people of Sabiliyat used to tell. In the days of the monarchy, before the second world war had yet broken out, the chief of some tribe from the Al-Qarna region came to visit accompanied by his childless wife. The wife submitted her vow, she'd give ten sheep as a gift if God was gracious to her and granted her a child. At some point during their visit, his wife wanted to perform the ritual ablution. He saw there was a crude-looking reservoir of water that stood at the bottom of a short flight of steps carved out of the trunk of a palm tree. The reservoir was fed by a small creek that had only a trickle of water in it. He suddenly resolved to make a vow of his own. "If the Almighty answers my wife's prayers, I'll build a proper pool for people to drink."

It was said that the wife got pregnant and gave birth to twins, a girl and a boy. When it was time to fulfill the vow, the husband decided he would build a pool that was worthy of the shrine. He bought the palm tree orchard that lay at the back of the shrine and annexed to the shrine as a religious endowment. He dug out the small creek and turned it into a pond that fed into a large pool made of cement, with broad marble steps leading down to it. He had the surrounding land planted with blackberry bushes, interspersed with shrubs of damask rose. As the years went by, people let the condition of the pool slip, but nevertheless it remained a landmark with a special connection to the shrine.

Coming up before the pool, she felt a sense of bitterness well up in her. The marble steps lay under a blanket of brown dust. For a fleeting moment she had the impression she could hear the sound of frogs croaking somewhere. The bottom of the pool was also coated in dust. She felt an urge to follow the staircase down and head to the spot where the pool met the pond. A muddy patch of ground with just a dribble of stagnant water left in it. A current of joy suddenly went through her. She saw the heads of three frogs peeping out of the muddy surface. Not wishing to disturb them, she stepped carefully away. The thought flashed through her. *In a few days the mud that's left will have dried up. These frogs are in danger of dying.*

"Oh, Good Omen." She knows her Good Omen, he won't answer back, but she needs to share her distress with someone. "Here's our second morning nearly over, only eight days left. What can we do to stop all this dying or to hold it off a little?" A sense of anger gathered in her breast. "Fight each other to your heart's content, but why the water?"

She made it back to her house a little before sunset. She took out one of the parts of the noble Qur'an, squatted down opposite the open grave, and began reciting out loud. When she was done the night had fallen. She then addressed herself to her husband. "Twice now you've visited me carrying the axe of Deaf Abboud. What is it you're trying to tell me?" She listened carefully for a few seconds. "What good is it arming oneself with a carpenter's axe to demolish a dam several times higher than our house?" She felt a humid breeze brush against her face coming from the direction of the Shatt. She noticed the darkness had grown deeper. She lifted her eyes to the sky and saw that grey clouds had begun to coalesce just above her head. It came to her that this was the season of thunderstorms and sudden downpours. If it rained hard it might keep the earth nourished for days.

After a moment's silence, she resumed her exchange with her husband's remains. "When you visited me in my dreams here I didn't take your words seriously. The idea of waiting until the tide reaches its highest point and then digging a channel…" she trailed off. "During our life together, whenever I'd go overboard repeating some of the chatter I heard you'd smile reproachfully and say, 'People shouldn't say things that insult their intelligence.' I was of a mind to throw your words back at you now, except that your visit inside the shrine of Sayyid Rajab couldn't be a silly dream that means nothing." She shut her eyelids. She found the words of her son Saleh drifting back to her, about the tide reaching its peak when the moon became full on the midnight of the fourteenth, and also on the midnight of…Something like a spark suddenly went off inside her head. Tonight it was the twenty-eighth of Jumada Awwal, which meant that the tide would be reaching its peak on the Shatt at…She broke off her succession of thoughts. "I pray to God for protection from the Accursed."

The words of Second Lieutenant Sadeq suddenly came back to her. "The Iranians take the Nowruz festival very seriously and they stop fighting…" There were eight days left in the truce. She had the same number of days left there. There was something uncanny in the thought that the bombs would start falling on the place again just as the hour struck for her to leave. The image of the three frogs sitting inside the muddy bed of the pond at Sayyid Rajab's floated up before her. It wouldn't be their fate to survive.

A gleam of lightning tore across the northern horizon. She heard a rumble of thunder coming from afar, followed by what sounded like a donkey braying in the distance. Could that

97

be Good Omen? She hurried to the pen and peered inside. He wasn't there. Having stifled his desire to bray for several days, he must have needed to give vent to it. A second peal of thunder came accompanied by the same braying. Half an hour later the sound of Good Omen's snorting let her know he was back. "Who can blame you?" she said to him. The darkness thickened as a light drizzle began to fall. A sense of alarm came over her. Bu Qasem's grave. She brought out a piece of tarpaulin and draped it over the open top of the grave to stop the water from seeping in. "The water coming from the sky is a blessing, but I don't want you to get wet," she said to him. The lightning gleamed across the sky several more times and the thunder grew louder as the rain began to beat down. Around ten o'clock she headed to bed.

"Where is the axe?" She was quick to disclaim. "I don't know." Bu Qasem's bewilderment was beyond bounds. "I put it at the edge of the bed a short while ago." She didn't try to disguise her sense of displeasure. "What will you do with the axe?" "You know full well," he said in a chiding tone. She must have begun entreating him. "Please explain to me." She couldn't make out his reply. She heard a terrible roar. Who was to say the war hadn't...Her senses went on high alert. She sat up bolt upright and opened her eyes inside the darkness of the room. Let it be good, oh Lord. The world around her responded with a crash of thunder that was followed by pounding rain. Her spirits settled a little. Their war hadn't...She ran over her dream in her mind. Bu Qasem and his stubborn insistence on the axe. There was no one else in Sabiliyat but her. *Meaning, I'm the one responsible, whatever the repercussions.*

She went out to the courtyard. The rain was at its fiercest,

98

and the lightning kept being followed by thunder or signaling its next peal. She saw Good Omen standing at the entrance of the pen ready to accompany her. The idea of trying to shield herself from the rain didn't even cross her mind. The whole of nature was welcoming the rain with open arms. It didn't take her long to get the axe in hand. She couldn't rule out the possibility of repercussions arising that would have to be accounted for before…She could barely begin to imagine the form the punishment would take, but she had an immediate sense of doing something that went against the soldiers' conventions.

The road had entirely surrendered to the rain. Good Omen stood still waiting for her to mount him. "Later," she said to him. She began walking at a brisk pace while he resigned himself to trotting alongside her. She turned into an alley on the right and following it along she reached a wooden bridge that ran across Sayyid Rajab River. She came to a halt. Good Omen halted at her side waiting for her next move. "Let's go down," she said to him. She was the first to make it to the bottom. He cautiously steadied himself with his hooves as he went down the steep slope to avoid slipping until he finally came to a halt beside her. She stroked his neck before climbing onto his back. "Let's head for the dam."

Good Omen made his way along the trench of the river. In a few minutes they were standing at the base of the towering dam. She dismounted. "Not a sound," she whispered admonishingly. She began scaling the side of the dam. The earth had become slippery from the amount of rainwater it had soaked up, and she had to use the axe for balance. Coming up to the top, she popped her head over the dam. As the lightning lit the sky, she could see the tents of the soldiers being lashed by the rain behind the row of date palm trees. *They're sheltering inside them.* Her gaze traveled over to the Shatt. She saw it surging with tidewater, thirstily drinking in the rain that was pouring down. Her heart skipped with love. She continued going until she had made it to the very top.

To be on the safe side, she decided to crawl along the top of the dam on her belly until she made it to the other end where the Shatt was. She was astonished to see how high the water came up. There were no more than a few inches separating the surface of the water from the top of the dam. She immediately fell to work with the axe. What she needed to do was dig a small channel and slowly draw the water of the Shatt toward her. Her body heaved backward from the effort as she pulled away at the mud. The water of the Shatt responded and began to drift toward her. She wasn't disturbed by the crashing thunder and the rain that was pounding down ever harder.

Within half an hour she had reached the interior side of the dam. She felt a rush of joy as she saw the water of the Shatt beginning to wend its way into the dry trench of Sayyid Rajab River. For a few seconds she followed the moving water with her eyes. It was true, water had its own special way of perceiving things. There it was, carving out its channel ever wider and deeper, sweeping the soil along as it went. She was almost certain sooner or later it would wash away part of the dam. She climbed onto Good Omen's back. "Let's head back." As she retraced her steps she was quiet in her mind that the water of the Shatt would be able to make it into her dry river. Yet that still left another river standing dry. "Let's go to our watering spot." Good Omen responded by breaking into a gallop. The sky over Sabiliyat was still pouring down rain.

100

Um Qasem set about putting the same plan into execution for a second time. Arriving at the base of the dam on Chouma River, scaling the side, reaching the top, digging out a small channel. This time she worked faster, out of a fear lest the water of the Shatt should start to ebb. As she was buckling down to work, she heard shouts coming from the camp and she saw the soldiers running toward the dam on Sayyid Rajab River. Maybe it had been the roar of the water as it burst powerfully forth, sweeping the soil along on its course. As long as they kept busy over there she was safe. She smiled to herself. Soon they'd hear the roar of the water coming from here. She began to dig. The soil of the dam had grown even softer as a result of the falling rain, enabling her to finish her work rapidly. The water began to pour out as she was mounting Good Omen's back. "Let's go home," she whispered to him. She strained her ears to listen to the surroundings. The only thing to be heard were the continuing shouts of the soldiers. She made out the voice of Lieutenant Abdel Kareem. "We need more sandbags!" Her smile broadened. Boosting the dam with sand at a time of high tide would only increase the amount of water the river absorbed.

The rain grew lighter until finally it stopped. She glanced up at the sky. The clouds were beginning to disperse. A strong northern gust blew in. The weather was clearing. She felt a slight tingling inside her nose. May God protect us. She started to sneeze. She needed to get home as quickly as possible and make herself some ginger tea to avoid catching a cold. As she stepped through the door, she cast a glance at the piece of tarpaulin that lay over the open top of the grave. She didn't need to fill Bu Qasem in on what she'd accomplished. He

101

knew it all already. Her exhaustion was so great she put the idea of ginger tea aside and headed straight to bed.

Bu Qasem had never taken her on a trip like this before. They were sitting opposite each other inside a small skiff. It was Sayyid Rajab River, and the tide was at its highest. It suddenly occurred to her to ask him, "Where are you taking me?" He gave her a loving smile. "To the Apple Field." She didn't try to disguise her alarm. "We haven't asked its owner for permission." His grin grew broader. "Just you stay with me," he said like one seeking assurances before continuing, "We won't meet any opposition." She felt like asking, "Why is that?" But he went on, "You're one of a kind." She had a sense she'd heard that expression somewhere before. Bu Qasem's next words took her by surprise. "Even though he's always in a uniform, Lieutenant Abdel Kareem has a good heart in him." She was distracted by the tingling in her nose and the need to sneeze. She shuddered awake.

As her dream melted away, a sense of loss took its place. Bu Qasem was dead. Her ears picked up the sound of Good Omen snorting. She opened her eyes. Reality in all its bewildering complexity. Upon getting out of bed, she found Good Omen standing before her. The late morning sun was filling the courtyard. She heard the sound of knocks on the door.

9

"I'VE BEEN KNOCKING FOR A WHILE." There was a smile on Second Lieutenant Sadeq's face. "The only thing I could hear inside was the snorting of the donkey."

"I didn't get to sleep until the break of dawn," Um Qasem explained apologetically. "All that lightning and thunder and pounding rain," she went on. She motioned toward her nose. "And this cold on top—"

"Lieutenant Abdel Kareem requests your attendance."

"Nothing wrong, I hope?"

"I'm not sure what he wants exactly."

She kept her eyes on his face, hoping he would say more.

"I believe he wants to ask you some questions," he said.

"What about?" she asked, trying to hide her apprehension. Maybe he felt sorry for her. "About what happened yesterday."

"Only the Great Almighty has control over the rain," she said with resignation.

"It has to do with the collapse of the two dams."

She packed every last ounce of astonishment into her voice. "How did that happen?"

They began walking along. Good Omen quickly caught up with them. Um Qasem turned around to him and said,

"You can go get a bite to eat." Good Omen wheeled around and started back. Second Lieutenant Sadeq could not suppress his amazement.

"Your donkey understands you."

"Sometimes," she replied. "You must have an idea what kinds of questions Lieutenant Abdel Kareem wants to ask me…"

"I don't."

"Does he suspect anyone?"

"I believe he suspects sabotage."

"Who could do such a thing?

"It must be one of the enemies."

"Why one of the enemies?"

For a moment, he was at a loss how to respond. "These dams were built to prevent frogmen from infiltrating."

"Frog what?"

"Soldiers trained to dive over long distances."

She didn't say to him, *"I don't follow."*

He heaved out a melancholy sigh. "It's their shells that get us, not their frogmen."

Lieutenant Abdel Kareem was sitting inside his tent. She noticed he was scowling.

"Good morning."

"Hi," he shot back curtly.

A sense of alarm coursed through her. It flashed through her mind that maybe he knew something about her exertions the previous night.

"Where's your husband?"

She managed to fight off her bewilderment. "At home… in the pit," she added, clarifying.

"At home, or in the pit?" he challenged her, suspiciously.

She stiffened for a few moments. The sense of injury was evident in her voice. "Don't be upset if I say you're confusing me." She continued plaintively, "What do you want from me?"

"The truth," he answered dryly.

"What truth?" she asked, in an injured tone.

"Who did you bring with you?"

"Good Omen."

"I'm talking people."

"Nobody."

"I suspect there's a whole gang of them out there."

"Where?"

He brushed off her question. "At your instigation they took it upon themselves to destroy the dams."

"You're being unfair to me." She was overcome by dismay.

"My suspicions come from words out of your own mouth."

"I swear by God Almighty that I only came with Good Omen."

He fixed her with a piercing look. "What you said about your husband and the axe he'd use to demolish—"

"You mean when he visited me in my dreams," she cut in.

"There has to be a link between intent to act and the perpetration of an act." She wished she could say to him, *"I don't follow."*

"It's only a matter of time before we identify the perpetrators."

"God willing," she muttered fervently.

"If we discover you had knowledge…" His voice grew fierce as he thundered out his threat. "If we discover there's a connection between you and saboteurs operating incognito…"

Again she wished she could say to him, *"I don't follow."*

His tone didn't soften. "My guess is you're pretending not to understand."

Her hand shot out involuntarily, as if to wave his voice away from her.

"Why are you doing that?" he demanded.

Her body gave a little sway but she regained her balance in time to stop herself from falling.

"I'm tired," she mumbled faintly and went down on her knees, hugging her body to herself.

He studied her with his eyes for a few seconds. Did it suddenly strike him that he had gone too far in accusing this poor old woman? He heaved out a sigh of resignation.

"You may go."

On exiting the tent, she turned left. The dam on Sayyid Rajab River was only a few dozen meters away from where she stood. She concentrated her gaze in that direction. She noticed the dam was now lined with sandbags along the top. They had replaced the soil with sand, thereby trapping the water that had flowed into the river and preventing it from returning to the Shatt during the ebb. This makeshift ploy of theirs had ensured the land would have water for weeks to come. When this time was over, Um Qasem couldn't be confident that another miracle would occur. There was no guarantee she'd be able to extend her stay past the Nowruz festival.

On her way back she was met by Good Omen. "Let's go see how our three little frogs are doing," she said to him. She thought it best to mount him. Her cold hadn't begun to relent yet, and combined with Lieutenant Abdel Kareem's interrogation she felt her forces had been depleted. She had to credit him for his acumen, but she hadn't committed any crime for which she deserved to be held accountable, unless the desire to preserve life should be counted a crime. Intuition told her that he still considered her a possible accomplice, though he didn't take the possibility seriously that the axe might have been the instrument used or that she might have acted alone without help from male accomplices. That was because he had no idea about the power that water was able to unleash when it was a matter of being true to its nature.

"God be praised!" she cried out as her eyes fell on the pool and she saw it was up to the brim with water. She slipped off Good Omen's back and hurried toward the water. She leaned over, scooped up a palmful of water, and washed her face before raising her eyes to the sky. "Praise and thanks be to you, oh Lord, for guiding me to do—" She stopped mid-sentence and started over. "Praise be to you for protecting me from the suspicions that got into Lieutenant Abdel Kareem's mind." She turned toward Good Omen and saw him bend over the water and start drinking in great big gulps. Her eyes scanned the surface of the pool. "Where are our three little frogs?" Her own delighted laughter caught her by surprise as it shook her body. All along the wall of the pool she could see dozens of frogs of varying sizes lined up with only their heads visible above the water. She strained her ears hoping she might catch the sound of one them croaking…Nothing happening just then. "You're all safe now." As she began to move away, she heard one of them breaking into a croak followed by a whole chorus.

She crossed the graveyard and came up before the river. It was looking closer to being full. The water was a dark green, shading into brown. Even though the long absence of water had wiped out the fruit trees, there was comfort in the fact that the date palms and Christ's-thorn trees would soon be able to recover their strength. She turned toward Good Omen. He understood what was turning in her mind. He drew up to her and she climbed onto his back. "Let's go home."

He rode along at an easy pace. He knew his mistress needed time to take in the surroundings with all their particulars. To the left of the paved road stood the house of Yaseen Abdel Khidr, who was known around the village by the nickname "Boy-Daddy." After he was married, he had one boy born to him, then a second and a third and yet a fourth, and all the while he kept dreaming of a little baby girl. It took nine boys before the girl finally came along, a great beauty the spitting image of her mother.

They drew up alongside Sabry's walled garden, which gave onto the grounds of his house. She caught a glimpse of the large rolling fronds of the Khisab date palm tree, known among the villagers for the delicious juicy black fruit it produced into the middle of winter. Next to Sabry's house was Mahmoud's, followed by Sabhan's, followed by Abdel Muhsin's, with its Barhee date palm in the middle of the courtyard. Fahd's came up after that, and then it was Abdallah's at the far end. Six houses belonging to six brothers, all of them scattered by the war along with their families. Were she to enter any one of these houses, she'd be able to access all of the rest through openings in the internal walls or by following the interconnected roofs.

She wasn't at her house yet when she was surprised to see Second Lieutenant Sadeq standing before her.

"I got here half an hour ago."

108

"Nothing wrong, I hope?"

He smiled sweetly and held out something sizable that was wrapped in paper.

"What is this?"

"Six pieces of army bread," he replied. "Lieutenant Abdel Kareem's orders," he added.

Her eyes sparkled with gratitude. "That's too much," she muttered. His gesture made it impossible to doubt his good intentions, she thought to herself.

The successful accomplishment of purpose brings clarity to the mind. On the following morning, her thoughts returned to the courtyard of Mahmoud Abbas's house and to the dry bed of roses in particular. What were the odds she could get hold of some live shoots to plant? Her mind flew back to the thicket of rose shrubs she'd seen on the bank of the Shatt, at the far end of a sprawling orchard called Al-Halabi's, belonging to the Naqeeb family. The orchard stood ten minutes away to the South. Going there meant walking past the tents of the soldiers. She weighed the alternatives in her mind. The cannon shells were still abiding by the Nowruz timetable, so there was no reason not to go have a look around.

Good Omen took her by the army camp first. Lieutenant Abdel Kareem was sitting in his chair looking out toward the Shatt. In a few days' time he'd no longer be able to do that.

"I'm on my way to an orchard nearby," she told him with the air of someone asking for permission.

"Be careful of unexploded shells," he cautioned her.

As she crossed the dam on Sayyid Rajab River, memories of what had recently taken place here came alive. The rain, the axe of Deaf Abboud. Her face was brushed by fresh gusts of wind drifting across from the rolling expanse of the water. She drew in a deep breath that filled her chest. Good Omen suddenly stopped short, his eyes fixed on a patch of ground right before him. She followed his gaze and saw a hideously deformed hole with a strange metal object sticking out. "God is our keeper." She didn't need to instruct him. He swerved to the side steering clear of the periphery of the hole. "Take your time," she said to him.

She couldn't tear her eyes from the Shatt. Those waters stretching out into the horizon, the gentle rippling of the surface. It would be an entirely different picture if the wind picked up. She could see the spot where Al-Halabi's orchard made a slight projection into the Shatt. Memories from the time of her youth revived in her mind. They called that projection "Al-Halabi's Jetty." The land there made a drop that was deep enough for the owls coming from Kuwait during the date harvest season to perch on it. Her senses picked up a perfumed scent. She focused her gaze. Shrubs of damask rose sat densely clustered along part of the embankment just where it sloped toward the water.

10

THE WINDS TRACED OUT SHIFTING FORMS as they grazed the face of the Shatt. She used her sickle to steady herself, taking care not to slip on the spongy ground. She picked out four shrubs of damask rose growing on the part of the bank that was soaked in water. She set to work cutting their long branches, making sure she pulled them up together with their soil and doing her best to preserve as many of their roots as she could. With a bit of luck, these shoots would be blooming within weeks. The natural cascade of her thoughts brought a pang of sorrow. But they'll be at risk of dying from thirst unless they find someone to water them regularly after I'm taken away.

Her mind fell to work for a few moments. During this time she finished hitching the shoots to Good Omen's saddlebags. She suddenly found herself saying out loud, "I have to stay." She hadn't endured the hardships of the journey and confronted the dangers of the way over from Najaf only to resign herself to being expelled. She reflected for an instant. "What's to be done, Bu Qasem?" She was speaking to him as if he were right there listening. "You won't abandon me," she continued with appeal. After a moment's silence she came out with what sounded like a proposal. "You show me what I have to do." The sequence of her thoughts was arrested by the honks of a flock of geese crossing the sky overhead. She looked up. These birds were masters of the air. Her eyes traveled to a date palm tree that used to tower to a great height. Its neck had taken a direct hit from a passing shell, and it had snapped to one side. Its head had rolled sideways under the burden of its heavy crown of leaves, and frozen in midair in that position it had shriveled away. It was a sight as paining as it was shameful. The shells were also masters of the air.

On her way back she ran into Second Lieutenant Sadeq who was walking along with one of his soldiers. He greeted her warmly and betrayed a curiosity at the sight of the damask rose shoots. "Where will you plant them?" Before she had a chance to answer he shot out again in a wondering tone, "What's the point of planting them unless someone can take care of them?"

His question recalled her to the prospect of her expulsion in a few days' time. She suddenly found her reply. "God bless your helping hands."

He straightened and said with spirit, "I'm at your service."

Good Omen led the way into Mahmoud Abbas's house and they followed.

"I can take care of your seedlings if you wish," the other soldier offered eagerly.

She smiled at him. "What's your name?"

"Jasem."

"God keep you, Jasem."

After the damask rose shoots had been planted, Um Qasem said to them, "I'll need your help." She was thinking she could use their help to repair the parapet of the mosque which had been damaged by a shell.

112

As she came up to the watering spot on the back of her house, her spirits rose. Chouma River was brimming with water. Good Omen darted ahead and bent over. His present enthusiasm was worlds apart from the displeasure he'd shown on the morning of their arrival. The ground of the courtyard was still wet from the rain of the previous day. She pulled back the tarpaulin from over the grave and sat down facing the pit. "I finished planting the roses at Mahmoud Abbas's. I forgot to bring back a seedling just for you to plant by your head." Her attention was caught by a laughing dove that was rustling about in the date palm. She smiled with contentment. She went back to addressing her husband. "I promise you I'll bring you two seedlings." She then qualified. "On condition you tell me how to extend my stay here." She was silent for a moment. "The soldiers are going through a phase they call a truce. They say it will end on the day of the Nowruz festival. I don't know what things will be like after that. I've seen the shells of cannons, I don't know what kind of fear might come into me if I stay here while the bombing is going on. I don't think I'll get so scared I have to leave." Her voice shimmered with love. "If they force me to go I'll take you with me."

She thought it wise to inform Lieutenant Abdel Kareem. "I saw a hole with one of their shells inside."

He asked her if it was exploded.

"I don't know."

Second Lieutenant Sadeq and Sergeant Fawzi were assigned to accompany her. "This is our explosives expert," the former introduced them.

She led them to the location. After cautiously inspecting the metal object Sergeant Fawzi announced, "We'll need to detonate it at the spot." She didn't dare to ask how. "It's a good thing you didn't try lifting the shell out," Second Lieutenant Sadeq said to her. She made no answer. Ever since she'd gotten there, she'd been expected to catch on to everything happening around her.

The three of them retraced their footsteps together. "Sergeant Fawzi will oversee the detonation of the shell at a later point in time," Second Lieutenant Sadeq explained to her. After the other had gone off he said to her with suppressed pain, "Our previous explosives expert was killed during the performance of his duties." What could she read into this, she listened as he went on. "His shredded limbs were found scattered dozens of meters from the site of the explosion." *There are ways of dying one can hardly conceive, she thought to herself.*

As they were walking along, he suddenly pointed ahead. "There's Good Omen waiting for you." She looked up and saw her donkey standing at the entrance of a lane leading to an open area that formed part of Sayyid Zayd Al-Naqeeb's mansion. He gave a toss of his head before disappearing into the lane. Something must have caught his interest. She stepped up her pace, her companion followed suit. As they reached the top of the lane, she saw Good Omen chewing at some stalks of grass in the middle of what looked like a graveyard just behind where the soldiers' tents stood. There were four rows of gravestones laid in parallel. She was dumbfounded.

"In our time these graves didn't use to be here. This is no place for a graveyard," she reproached him. "Do you bury your dead right in the middle of your tents?"

"It's not like that," he responded quickly. "According to military regulations, the army is required to deliver the bodies of the fallen to their families," he explained.

Her sense of shock wasn't abating.

"Master Sergeant Abdel Bari was the one who came up with the idea," he went on. "When one of our men was killed over two years ago, he decided to bury one of the shirts belonging to that soldier. He then planted a gravestone over it with his name so he could continue to live on among us."

A bitter taste gathered in Um Qasem's mouth. Only moments ago her companion had been telling her about the scattered limbs of one of their men.

They were sitting across from each other inside a boat swaying along the waters of the Shatt al-Arab. It was just before sunset, and the Shatt was packed with boats as far as the eye could see. Everyone was in a festive mood as if there was something special happening. There were people playing music, people singing and dancing, happy shouts ripping through the air from every direction. Suddenly she realized this was the day of the festival, the day of Nowruz. A sense of disorientation came over her, because she was certain the day of Nowruz had not arrived yet.

Bu Qasem signaled to her. "What's wrong?" She thought she'd share her sense of confusion with him. "There's a mistake." He gave a wry laugh. "There are many mistakes." She couldn't find anything to say in response. She had the sense she'd experienced this kind of scene before. They were sitting inside a smaller boat on Sayyid Rajab River, which was swollen with tidewater, and there was no one else nearby. Suddenly people's voices grew louder all around them. She couldn't distinguish the cries of joy from the cries of terror. A chill ran through her, the fear of something unknown that was about to swoop down. "Let's go home," she said to him. His silence felt interminable. "We will." "When?" she urged him. Once more she had to endure his silence. "When the time is right."

Her consciousness was playing games with her. It shut out the throngs of people and their shouts and began hurtling after a sequence of images and memories belonging to a time that seemed to float free of everything. A colossal mud dam, small army tents that looked like they were buried in the ground. Metal objects splintered along the edges, date palm trees with their shriveled crowns dangling to one side. Bu Qasem bored into her thoughts. "It's because they live in the middle of their graves," he explained. Her mind sparked off. "Their graves have no bodies inside," she said. He sighed in sorrow. "It's a sad thing." She knew her answer. "I won't abandon your remains as long as I live." He smiled at her lovingly. "That will be given to you." Unbroken silence reigned, then the details of the scene quickly faded away. She was standing alone in the middle of a vast empty land that was lined with gravestones as far as the eye could see. She was gripped by terror. Why me? Despite the disorientation she felt, it occurred to her to reprimand herself. "I have to stop…"

She sat up bolt upright. The dark of the night, the room, the bed. Let it be good, oh God. She was still for an instant. She turned her senses inward. There was a weight of radiant yearning for the one who was absent yet present. Suddenly she had the sense she'd been negligent. She had failed to take advantage of the opportunity to ask him for advice. How could she persuade those soldiers to let her stay? But then she ran over the sequence of her dream in her mind. Bu Qasem had communicated his message on this point when he said, "That will be given to you." She looked toward the half-open door. The light of dawn was beginning to spread outside. She wouldn't be getting back to sleep. Her imagination quickened as some of the details of her dream came back to her. Why had Bu Qasem chosen the Nowruz holiday? They'd never taken a boat together before on an occasion like this.

She remembers him taking her down to the waterfront one Nowruz before she got pregnant with their first son Qasem. The coast swarming with people, the Shatt swarming with boats all the way from Al-Maqam Bridge down to Al-Khoura Bridge. The singing, the dancing, the festive mood all around. That was the time when the monarchy was still standing. Following the July 14 Revolution, the day of Nowruz had been transformed over the years into a simple herald of the start of spring.

"Oh Bu Qasem, when will we be able to live without fear?" She was still for a moment. Even if the prospect of her departure was sealed, she had to make good use of the few days that remained. "Let's go." Good Omen sprang into motion and fell in step behind her. It occurred to her that it might be worth having a look around the house of Jawad Al-Daleeshi, Mahmoud Abbas's next-door neighbor. As chance would have it, this pair of close neighbors had ended up marrying each other's sisters and had become uncles to one another's children. At some point they had knocked down part of the wall separating the courtyards of their houses.

She entered Mahmoud Abbas's house with Good Omen following on her heels. She examined the damask rose seedlings from every side. All of their leaves still looked green and strong.

She saw Good Omen gingerly bring his snout to the spray of one of the seedlings. "No." He turned his head away obediently. He led the way into the courtyard of Jawad Al-Daleeshi's house. There was another oversized Christ's-thorn tree growing there that was known for the fleshy fruit it produced, which was among the first to ripen and could be eaten with the entire pip. The ground of the courtyard was carpeted with dry leaves that had fallen from the Christ's-thorn tree. Those leaves were set apart by a distinctive perfume they possessed. The mistress of the house, Um Hadi, would regularly collect them and pack them into a range of similar-sized paper bags at the behest of several women in the village who'd use them for their wash. Good Omen briskly trotted over and buried his snout into the leaves hoping to unearth some nabk fruit. She lifted her eyes to the tree. It stung her to see its branches all dead save for the ones growing nearest the trunk. The water basin, the tap, the familiar whistle before the water came sputtering out.

Her eyes drifted to the half-open door of the kitchen. The door of the dry goods storeroom stood right next to it. Not now. She decided instead to take a look at the courtyard at the rear of the house, which connected to an extensive orchard that reached all the way up to the bank of Sayyid Rajab River. A sense of vexation rose up in her as her eyes fell on the rear wall. Two shells had struck it in close proximity, leaving it mutilated. Inside the rear courtyard there were two towering Barhee date palms as well as a mass of intersecting branches belonging to three orange trees and some bougainvillea shrubs which were now brittle and bare. The date palms were the solace.

She turned to Good Omen. "Let's go." He fell in step behind her. She crossed a wide gate and came up before the open sprawl of the orchard. A smile of contentment broke over her face. The creeks were brimming with water. The orchard was called Um Al-Barhee because it contained fifty date palm trees of the Barhee variety, all of which came up to the exact same height, five meters. Before the July 14 Revolution the orchard had formed part of the estate of the Naqeeb family, like most other assets in the area. But with the conditions turning after the revolution and with many of the legatees emigrating abroad, the orchard had been put up for sale. Jawad Al-Daleeshi had stepped forward and paid the asking price. At the time he had said that his grandfather on his father's side had been the original proprietor of Um Al-Barhee.

Um Qasem knew there used to be a row of giant desert poplars studded all along the bank of Sayyid Rajab River. She was hoping to herself that she wouldn't find the desert poplars dead. She was aware that this type of tree required a steady supply of water. She quickened her pace. Desert poplars were a type of willow with a delicate constitution and they were easily damaged. She saw the branches lying in heaps around what remained of the tree trunks. By the time Sayyid Rajab River had swelled with water, it was already too late for the poplars. "Let's go." Was it that he picked up on her sadness, she wondered, as Good Omen walked quietly by her side with a stooped head.

11

"EVEN THOUGH YOU'VE ONLY BEEN with us ten days, we'll definitely miss you," Lieutenant Abdel Kareem said in an affable tone.

Um Qasem didn't share with him what was turning in her thoughts. *If only you could forget I'm even here.*

"Be packed and ready to leave this time tomorrow," he went on.

A one-way conversation that took place a little before noon on the twenty-first of March.

"To make things easy for you, I've asked the driver of our supply truck to take you and your donkey up to the border of the province."

The sense of grief that washed over her at that moment made it impossible for her to reply. All she could do was nod in assent. Did he intuit the causes of her listlessness? He concluded the exchange with an air of reluctant resignation.

"Things are not up to us."

On the same afternoon, she received a visit from Second Lieutenant Sadeq and Private Jasem. The former sought to put her mind to rest.

"I'll make sure your rose seedlings get watered."

"You're a good soul," she answered gratefully.

"All these kind words you keep showering on us," Private Jasem protested.

She gave a sad smile. "May it please God to bring this war to an end."

After they had left, she went up to the open grave. "Be prepared, it seems we'll be going away tomorrow." She then qualified, "Unless you see things differently." She tensed for a moment as if waiting for some kind of reaction to come before continuing. "I know you don't want to leave, I don't want to either. Lieutenant Abdel Kareem says things are not up to them, I didn't understand why." She tensed again for a little longer and then asked, "What do you think?"

Time ticked by in a state of tension unlike anything she'd ever experienced before. A sense of helplessness, coupled with a total inability to think logically. If they carried her off to the Basra border with Good Omen and her husband's remains, where would she go from there? Her mind couldn't adjust to the idea that she would simply retrace her steps back to where she came from. She was incapable of going back to that feeling of being superfluous that had tormented her there even though she was surrounded by her children and grandchildren. "What can we do?" She directed the question to Good Omen. He responded with a subdued snort. The sun had just set. "I think you realize it's our last night here."

She began feasting on the contents of her house with her eyes as if she was seeing everything for the first time. The sense of being under siege was making it harder to breathe. The pointlessness of it, to have made it home only to have to go away again, as if her whole life was at the mercy of decisions made by… The question that sprang up in her mind came as if out of nowhere. How would Lieutenant Abdel Kareem and the rest of the soldiers react if I went off, stayed away for a few days, and then came back? Perhaps they'd drive her out by force. She fell to thinking. I'm responsible for my own actions. Her decision was formed. *I'll set off tomorrow before sunrise.* It was better for her to go off that way instead of having to submit to their orders, not to mention the fact that she couldn't vouch for Good Omen and say how he'd take it if they tried to force him into their truck. She went to the pen and told him, "We get going at dawn." Her ears didn't register a response. Perhaps he was still feeling downhearted or confused.

Time crawled by, weighted with anxiety and anticipation. The sky looked pale even though it was a cloudless night. She went to bed around eleven o'clock. She needed to get a few hours' rest so she would be ready to travel. She'd just about dozed off when she was woken up by the sound of Good Omen braying. She had the impression he was standing right outside the door. A sense of anxiety swept over her. What's gotten into him? As she was about to climb out of bed, she was startled by a series of thundering explosions that rang out in close succession. This war by the look of it… She didn't get a chance to finish her thought. A sharp hiss tore through the air and the walls of her room shook as she felt the impact of a shell landing somewhere nearby. "Good Omen!" she cried out in terror. She ran to the door and looked outside. He wasn't there. She saw a billow of dust rising from a gash in the ground near Bu Qasem's grave. "Good Omen!" she called out panic-stricken. The sound of his low snorting reached her ears coming from the pen. She rushed over. He was cowering in the far corner. She came up to him. "You'll be okay, don't worry."

Their truce is over and now they're getting on with their war again, the thought flashed through her mind. She strained her ears toward the Shatt. The sound of cannons going off mingled with the whistling of shells coming from somewhere far away. It was not knowing what might happen in the next minute that made her freeze with fear. If only she could understand why all of this was happening. Minutes later a shell landed in the alley right outside the door of her house. It was followed by another shell that hit the house of Deaf Abboud. It was as if they were targeting this spot specifically for all the world. Strikes and counterstrikes continued without letup. These people don't even give one a chance to catch one's breath. It suddenly crystallized in her mind, the only place she'd be safe was at Sayyid Rajab's shrine. She roused Good Omen. "Let's go."

Ever since she can remember her own existence, she had never experienced anything like this. Starting wars had to be an act of human stupidity. As she raced along with her hand on Good Omen's neck to steady him, it seemed to her as if the way to the shrine had grown several times longer and as if the very air she was drawing into her chest had become hostile. When she'd finally made it, she decided to take shelter at the rear of the building. She slumped to the ground with her back against the wall. Good Omen halted a couple of steps away and stood by with stooped head. The exchange of fire eased and then ground to a stop. Dare she hope that...? The pause lasted a few minutes and then the bombardment picked up again at an escalating pace. One of the shells struck a branch at the top of the Christ's-thorn tree. The branch snapped off and crashed to the ground not far from where Good Omen was standing. Good Omen emitted a snort of protest. "May evil pass you over."

The bombing didn't stop for good until the light of dawn had begun to spread on the horizon. There's a heaviness to silence, your ears on the alert for a whistling sound which you hope will keep going overhead, the air still thick with the smell of burning. She waited until the morning light had grown a little stronger and then she headed for the pool. The pool was still up to the brim with water. Her eyes began searching for the frogs. She spotted a few of them clinging to the cement wall along the waterline. She tensed for a moment with her ear toward them. Not a peep to be heard. It seemed that the racket of the war reduced the frogs to silence. Her cheer rose a little as she caught sight of a hoopoe a few meters away. It was hopping about quickly without a moment's pause, almost flying off the ground. She figured it must be hungry. How was it able to get hold of the food it needed when it hardly stopped moving for two seconds at a time? Today was the twenty-second of March, which meant spring had begun. But the light coming from the sun was a pale yellow that struck gloom into the spirit. Suddenly a question shot through her mind. What about the soldiers stationed by the Shatt? The bombardment, its consequences…

Good Omen uttered a low snore and turned his head toward the opening that led into the passageway. She turned to look in that direction and saw Second Lieutenant Sadeq and Private Jasem approaching.

"Praise God you're safe!" the lieutenant cried out.

"We looked for you everywhere," Private Jasem said.

She broke in anxiously, "I hope none of you—" Words failed her.

"There were no casualties and no injuries," the lieutenant hastened to reassure her.

"Praise be to God," she said with relief. "It was a fierce war."

Private Jasem corrected her with a smile. "Real war involves meeting the enemy and clashing face to face. What happened was an ordinary case of reciprocal strikes."

If only she could ask what was ordinary about seeing death stand a hair's breadth away. She remembered an eventuality that now lay before her. A sense of sadness washed into her voice.

"Has the truck that will take me away arrived?"

"That's not why Lieutenant Abdel Kareem sent us," Private Jasem said. "He wanted to make sure you're okay."

"He's a kind soul."

Second Lieutenant Sadeq spoke up. "The supply truck hasn't come yet." He was silent for a moment. "No one knows how many casualties we've had."

A look of confusion appeared on her face. "You said there were no casualties and no injuries."

"This time around they bombarded us across all fronts," he replied. "The headquarters of our division's command north of Basra were taking a heavy pounding before we lost communication with them."

It flashed through her mind that it was now too late to carry out her plan to depart at dawn. She tried her best not to let her sense of disappointment show.

"When will the truck arrive?"

"Due to the loss of communications nobody knows," Second Lieutenant Sadeq replied.

She hesitated a little. "Perhaps it won't arrive today."

"A few months ago our communications were cut as a result of the bombing, and the supply truck was four days late," Private Jasem volunteered.

"Our units have never suffered such heavy bombing before," Second Lieutenant Sadeq pitched in.

She wished she could say, *"Good Omen and I were beside ourselves with fear."* She wished she could add, *"Were it not for the shrine of Sayyid Rajab we would have found no peace."*

"One of their shells fell inside the courtyard of my house just a few steps from Bu Qasem's grave," she said. "I haven't had a chance to have a look around Deaf Abboud's house since it was hit," she added. She was silent for a couple of moments, and then she wondered out loud in a troubled tone, "And what about all the other houses?"

Private Jasem couldn't disguise his astonishment. "Surely you're not planning to repair the houses that have—"

"God bless your helping hands."

Perhaps he felt a little embarrassed. "I'm at your service for anything you need."

"What's the point of repairing things while the bombing continues?" Second Lieutenant Sadeq asked.

She heaved out a pained sigh. "You answer bombing with bombing."

"That's what wars of attrition are like," he countered in a defensive tone. Her unthinking reply took him aback.

"I don't understand what you're trying to tire out."

He gave a low laugh. "You ask some serious questions."

She began by taking a look at Deaf Abboud's house.

The shell had landed right outside the door of the carpentry workshop, producing a hole that was more than a meter across. "Good Omen, come here." First to transport the metal thing with the splintered edges to the dump round the back of her house. She wouldn't be able to smooth the ground over using just the axe alone, she had to use a spade. Then came the turn of her own house. After she'd eliminated all visible effects of the bombing to the best of her ability, she borrowed a short-legged wooden chair from Deaf Abboud's carpentry workshop and planted it opposite the open pit of the grave. She sat down and recited the "Verses of Refuge" from memory. Then she started on her subject. "It was as if the gates of hell had opened when they began bombing us. I don't know how the soldiers were able to cope with it, sitting where they are by the Shatt. They tell you 'no casualties,' but then they put up a graveyard to bury things that belonged to their dead. I asked you for advice about how I can make it so I stay. Now that I've come face to face with death…It never occurred to me that Good Omen understands the meaning of death." She went on, "You know me, you know I hate the thought of leaving Sabiliyat. I hope we can stay in our home until our children and grandchildren return. Perhaps it won't be long before that happens." A pained sigh escaped her. She then repeated in a tone of resignation, "But now that I've come face to face with death…I'm not so sure."

Her expulsion from the area depended on the arrival of their supply truck. The complication that had arisen meant that the arrival of the truck now depended on factors outside the scope of their knowledge. On the previous day she'd made herself a promise to examine the contents of the kitchen and the dry goods storeroom in Jawad Al-Daleeshi's house. "Let's

127

go." Good Omen quickly caught up with her. The bed of the Christ's-thorn tree with the fleshy fruit still had traces of water in it from the watering she'd given it the day before. She lifted her eyes to the branches of the tree. "The more you get watered, the stronger you'll get."

She went up to the kitchen door and turned the handle. This room was even bigger than the one in the house next door. The advantages of wealth were plain to behold. The oversized ceramic jars and metal containers, the aluminium cupboards lining the walls. If it was only a question of her own sustenance, the supplies in this kitchen were enough to keep her going for years. She was pleased to discover a small amount of bean seeds that hadn't been infested by worms. She could see it in her mind's eye. The creeks of the Daleeshiya orchard or Um Al-Barhee brimming with water...all she needed to do was bury a few bean seeds closely spaced in the spongy soil near the waterline. Hope egged her on. *I'd see ripe green sprouts coming out within a week.* Beans didn't need constant attention to grow. A moment later her excitement had dissipated. She had no guarantee she'd still be there in a week's time.

She went out of the kitchen and headed for the dry goods storeroom. She stood there hardly believing her eyes. The stockpile of food essentials, which included cooking oil and several different kinds of pulses, far exceeded her expectations. A sense of sorrow swept over her. This extensive supply of food would go to waste if the owners of the house didn't return. Doing her best to surmount her sense of despondency, she went around the house taking a look at the other rooms. After she had finished her rounds, she found herself standing before the kitchen once again. Suddenly she wondered to herself, what if she were to do something a little different?

It was after two in the afternoon when she approached the tent of Lieutenant Abdel Kareem.

"What's this?" His surprise was plain as he held out his hands to receive a covered pot she was offering.

"It's something for your lunch," she replied.

"No doubt a Basran dish of some kind."

She nodded and said, "Because your supply vehicle didn't come today."

She pointed to the pot. "It's without extras."

"What do you mean 'extras'?"

"A dish without beef or fish or chicken inside."

He lifted the cover and the fragrance of the cooked food wafted up to him. "It smells delicious." He reached in, picked up a lump with his fingers, and rolled it in his mouth. "Did you bring this rice with you from Najaf?"

She smiled with mysterious gratitude. "Everything I need for cooking is here in our houses." She continued, "There's enough rice, flour, and other basics to last you for months."

He smiled at her gratefully. "We won't be needing all that."

Her heart told her that Lieutenant Abdel Kareem was an honest man who had treated her kindly so far. She felt a desire to ask him to let her stay for longer, but there was a chance he might refuse and he would then say to her, *"You're a manipulative woman."* She turned things over in her mind. One can anticipate the reactions of people one knows well, but things are different with soldiers, no one can predict what they might do.

12

A LITTLE BEFORE SUNSET Um Qasem heard a shell whistling over-head followed by the sound of cannon fire coming from the army camp. The exchange of fire continued for nearly half an hour before subsiding again, a break that lasted until the following evening.

"What good does this bombing do?" Um Qasem asked.

"Somewhere along the front there's an exchange of fire or a clash and other areas flare up after that," Second Lieutenant Sadeq explained.

"Why do they flare up like that?"

He smiled at her chidingly. "If you were in the army you'd be summoned for a disciplinary hearing."

She gave a little laugh. "You have a point."

Second Lieutenant Sadeq's smile gave way to warm laughter. "You're a wise woman."

She was about to object when he continued.

"There's a lot of depth in the things you say."

She couldn't think of anything to say in reply.

"You'll leave a big gap behind when you go away."

Again she couldn't think of anything to say. She only heaved out a melancholy sigh.

After a few moments' silence he said, "No news on the supply truck yet."

"It will get here tomorrow," she ventured.

"Probably not," he said carefully.

She fixed her eyes on him.

"We still haven't managed to make contact with our command," he added.

Shortly before midnight the bombardment between the two sides started up again. It went on for a few minutes and then died down. Going into Mahmoud Abbas' house late the next morning to have a look around, she was surprised to find Private Jasem there.

"Since I planted the rose seedlings, I'm making sure they get watered."

"God bless you."

"The supply truck won't be coming today," he took the opportunity to inform her.

She didn't try to disguise her scepticism. "Are you sure?"

"We haven't reestablished contact with our command yet," was his disconcerting reply.

A third day passed, then a fourth. The bombardment between the two sides went on in fits and starts. Late on the morning of the fifth day, Second Lieutenant Sadeq came to meet her.

"I've come at the behest of Lieutenant Abdel Kareem. You mentioned to him something about the existence of food supplies."

"That's correct," she said, "Follow me."

As they were making their way toward Jawad Al-Daleeshi's house she said in a questioning tone, "It seems the supply truck won't be arriving today."

He didn't answer directly. "We were finally able to make contact with our command today. They asked us to fend for ourselves."

131

She decided not to trouble him with any more questions about the activities of the army. As they drew up before the door of the dry goods storeroom inside the house she asked him, "What do you need?"

"Whatever's available." A broad grin spread over his face as he stepped inside. "That's a decent stockpile." As he was busily picking out in his mind the things he needed he confided to her, "This is the first time the supply truck hasn't been around for five days in a row." A sigh escaped him. "It might be a while longer before it comes."

Um Qasem thought it best to listen in silence.

"We have all but definite information that the heavy Iranian bombardment following the Nowruz festival inflicted substantial losses on our unit's command, to say nothing of the damage done to the bridges."

"God be our helper," Um Qasem murmured feelingly.

They got down to work inside the storeroom, and together they sifted out some rice, wheat flour, sugar, cooking oil, and lentils. "The only thing that's missing are the extras," Um Qasem said.

A look of incomprehension appeared on his face.

"Beef, chicken, fish," she clarified.

"Our soldiers would never dream of such luxuries," he responded.

Her small wooden chair, sitting before the gap in the grave. "Bu Qasem," she appealed to him, her voice shot through with sadness. "Tomorrow it will be two weeks from the day the bombing started." She drew a deep breath and held it in her chest for a few moments. "May God preserve us. Our soldiers say there

132

haven't been any casualties so far. No one knows when this war will come to an end." She heard the call of a laughing dove coming from the top of the Hilawi date palm. She raised her gaze. The returning water in the Sayyid Rajab and Chouma rivers and the myriad creeks that fanned out from them had begun drawing a few birds into the area. Yesterday she had caught a glimpse of some starlings among the branches of Mahmoud Abbas's Christ's-thorn tree. She was hoping she'd see more of them. Her face darkened with vexation. Yesterday she had also noticed a perceptible drop in the water levels at the Daleeshiya orchard. A few weeks more and the state of utter drought would reassert itself. She stared deep into the grave. "What's to be done?"

She couldn't tell how long she'd spent crouched before her large tray cleaning the fish that was piled up inside it with the help of a small knife. Her arms had grown heavy with fatigue. "This had better be the last one, Saleh," she muttered to herself petulantly. Her son didn't stop. Every few moments he would appear carrying fresh amounts of fish of varying shapes and sizes, and he would declare to her joyfully, "There's plenty to go around!" She heaved out in protest, "But I'm tired." He laughed heartily. "We have a surplus of fish in Sayyid Rajab River." She remembered him hauling out his nets before midnight, the need to seize the moment when the tide reaches its peak. He and his funny calculations. "Where's your father? Why isn't he back yet?" "He and my brother Qasem are working hard to gather the fish." Her mind wandered. It's not like Bu Qasem to be spending his time fishing.

Perhaps her awareness flagged for a moment, she saw Bu Qasem squatting down opposite her cutting the fish into pieces

133

with the help of a sickle. There was pleasure in her surprise. "It's the first time you've ever given me a hand with the house-work." He smiled with affection. "We'll have more than forty guests coming over." Her awareness flagged once more, and Second Lieutenant Sadeq came in. She saw him sitting before her busily tipping the pieces of fish into a cooking pot. There was no hiding the astonishment in his voice. "Our soldiers could never dream of such luxuries." His hands stopped work-ing. He lifted his head listening to something in the distance. "What is it?" The entire scene melted away with all its details, leaving the smell of fresh fish playing in her nostrils.

She sat up straight in her bed. Let it be good, oh God. She remained there in the dark without moving. Her ears picked up the rumble of cannon fire coming from a distance. She thought she sensed something rustling in the courtyard. Good Omen. She got up and opened the door and saw Good Omen standing before her. "You're not used to the war, poor dear." She reached out and petted his forehead. Then she turned her eyes toward the open pit of the grave. "I didn't follow the point." Her mind kept churning over the events of her dream. This fish now, she remembered what people said about dreams, lots of fish means something good coming soon. She brushed that interpretation aside. Nothing good could ever come in the middle of a war. The appearance of her son Saleh followed by her husband per-plexed her. Was it his passion for fishing? She could almost hear her son's voice. "I want fish on rice with tamarind sauce." Her mind drifted back to the image of Bu Qasem in the middle of the dream, his helping to cut the fish and also his remark about forty guests coming over. She was at a loss how to interpret these

particulars. The appearance of Second Lieutenant Sadeq compli-
cated things further. "Our soldiers could never dream…" There's
a connection there. She had to go see the Shatt at high tide.

Around midday she headed for the army camp. Lieutenant
Abdel Kareem received her warmly.

"We're grateful to you for supplying us with food."

"It's the people of Sabiliyat you should thank."

He smiled. "You're a blessing from God."

She hesitated for a moment. She pointed to the dam over
his shoulder. "I need to spend a bit of time there."

"Why?"

She hesitated again. "Bu Qasem visited me last night…"

He smiled. "Hopefully he wasn't carrying his axe this time."

She shook her head and clarified. "He was trying to tell
me something about the fish in Sayyid Rajab River."

Lieutenant Abdel Kareem could find nothing to say in reply.

She made it to the dam and stood facing the Shatt. The
tide was almost at its peak, the northward drift of the strings
of seaweed floating along the surface was slowing down. The
rippling of the water was so gentle that it was almost imper-
ceptible. A fresh wind grazed against her face. In years gone
by, the horizon would have been dotted with dozens of boats
out fishing hilsa, their nets immersed in the water, only the
buoys made of palm leaf stumps showing. To maximize their
catch, they'd bide their time until the tide began to ebb and
the hilsa started to swarm toward the South, driven along by
the receding water. There was nothing on the Shatt now, no
fishing boats or steamboats or…

She turned around to look at Sayyid Rajab River, its water was static. She peered a little farther into the distance. Her eyes picked up a light rippling motion that suggested the presence of something or other in the water, perhaps it was a fish or two. She let her eyes rest there for a few seconds. The surface of the water grew still. She turned back to the Shatt. The strings of seaweed floating on the surface were now motionless. The ebb was beginning. She turned back to look at the river. She now noticed ripples were steadily forming on the surface of the water right next to the dam. The rays of the midday sun were piercing the surface of the water and lighting up part of the riverbed. Her heart began to beat faster. She could see dozens of fish of varying shapes and sizes swimming about. The fish were looking for an escape route that would take them to the Shatt, as if they were trying to remember the way they'd come from.

She leaned in to look, following the movement of the fish with her eyes. They'd been trapped there for weeks. Every so often a fish would make a little leap out of the water and then plunge back in, what purpose could that serve? Her ears tensed, they brought back the sound of her mother's voice the way she used to scold her. "You have the heart of a fish." She was a young girl at the time, she hadn't met Bu Qasem yet. Her mother meant to say she had no memory. Um Qasem's intuition told her there was nothing without memory. Humans, animals, plants, water, even the walls of houses had a special memory of their own. A few minutes went by. The fish congesting behind the dam lost hope of finding a way into the Shatt and retreated to the interior. On her way back she informed Lieutenant Abdel Kareem of what she'd seen. "We'll have fish extras to eat."

- 13 -

IT WAS NEARLY NOON WHEN Um Qasem approached the soldiers' tents, followed by Good Omen. He had a linen sack strapped to his back that contained a cast net used for fishing. Second Lieutenant Sadeq came out to meet her accompanied by Private Jasem. He greeted her with pleasure.

"Lieutenant Abdel Kareem told me yesterday that you've promised us fish for dinner."

She didn't reply directly. Instead she pointed to the linen sack. "I need your help." The two men immediately communicated their eagerness. As soon as Private Jasem caught sight of the net with its hem of lead sinkers he cried out, "It's a cast net!" The other man asked him if he knew how to use it. "There's hardly a man in Al-Faw who hasn't tried fishing with a cast net," he replied proudly. As the three of them were heading toward the Sayyid Rajab dam, they were joined by Private Mazen.

Moments after the water of the Shatt began to ebb, the fish started milling about on the other side of the dam.

"That's too much," Private Mazen mumbled in disbelief.

"Say 'God be praised' instead," Second Lieutenant Sadeq rebuked him.

Private Jasem slipped his left-hand wrist into the coil of

a rope which connected to the inside of the net at the other end and gathered up the hems with the lead sinkers in his right hand. He arched backwards and then flung the net wide while holding fast to the end of the rope, so that it flew out and landed on the water near the dam. He waited for the lead sinkers to reach the bottom of the river and then he slowly began to pull the rope in. The large fish began thrashing about madly trying to free themselves from the net, but their fins became tangled in its mesh. After the entire net had been drawn out of the water, Second Lieutenant Sadeq exclaimed with emotion, "That's another one of Um Qasem's blessings!" The number of large fish topped twenty, each fish weighing more than a kilo.

"Let's put the small fish back into the water," she said to them. She thought for a moment. "We can cook the fish in Al-Daleeshi's house."

Nobody raised objections.

The following evening, she ran into Private Jasem.

"They've finished repairing the bridges and clearing the roads."

She realized the time for her departure had almost come. She tried not to let her sense of sorrow show. "When?"

He didn't catch her drift.

"When will the supply truck arrive?"

He pondered her question for a moment. "Our unit's command rang up Lieutenant Abdel Kareem to find out what our urgent needs are so they could get on top of them straight away, and he said we're doing fine for the moment."

"When is your supply truck coming?" she asked with impatience.

"I don't know."

Her mind staggering with sorrow, she traced her way home. "Oh Bu Qasem, even if you and I have no objection to traveling on their truck, what about Good Omen? How could he ever get into their truck of his own accord and keep calm for the entire journey?" Her ears picked up the cooing of a pigeon coming from somewhere inside the foliage of the Hilawi date tree. With her, everything was a matter of signs and intimations. The conviction took hold of her, Bu Qasem will visit me in my dreams and show me what to do. Suddenly the wind picked up. She heard a sound like a snore coming from the pen. Animals are better at noticing what's happening around them. The wind gathered strength, it began to storm. The air grew turbid with dust. She starting sneezing. This was no time for coming down with a cold. If she had to fall ill, it should be when circumstances were appropriate.

The storm eased up as the night wore on, which was more than could be said about Um Qasem's state. Head aching, nose running, sleep eluded her. If she could nap even for just an hour she'd feel better, she was almost certain of it. Lying all alone in the darkness, and this relentless grind of time. She couldn't tell how long it was before exhaustion finally got the better of her and she succumbed to sleep. *"If we discover you had knowledge…"* Despite the stern voice in which he was speaking, Lieutenant Abdel Kareem's kindness shone through his features. She heard him go on, *"Your presence will bring unwelcome inquiries down on our heads."* She was about to say, *"I'm aware of that,"* but he continued. *"You see in fact…we won't force you to leave."* She was dumbfounded. How could he both say she must leave and also that they won't compel her? She felt like asking him to clarify but he faded away.

Consciousness returned to her. She was lying stretched on her bed. Good Omen's low snorts reached her from the other side of the door. The light of day was spreading outside. She remembered the discomfort she'd been in before she dozed off, but her nose felt better now. She went over the details of her dream in her mind. It was Lieutenant Abdel Kareem on his own. If this was a message from Bu Qasem, why hadn't he showed up himself? Everything in its proper time, she reassured herself. She felt a pang of hunger. She hadn't had a bite to eat since noon on the previous day. She briskly made her way to the kitchen. As she was having breakfast, the decision came to her.

"God keep you, Um Qasem."

A sense of joy broke over her. This was the first time Lieutenant Abdel Kareem had greeted her this way. She lost no time making her announcement.

"We've decided to leave."

He was about to ask her to explain but she carried on.

"We don't want to cause you any more grief. Tomorrow morning at dawn Bu Qasem, Good Omen and I will depart."

Having delivered her message, she turned on her heels and began to walk away.

"Um Qasem," he called out.

She stopped in her tracks. She tried to hide the tears in her eyes before turning around to face him.

"We said we'd wait for the supply truck so you'd be spared some of the hardship of the long journey. What's the reason for this decision?"

"Even if Bu Qasem and I have no objections, I don't want to put Good Omen though this mortifying experience," she replied.

He suppressed a smile. "What experience?"

"I know him well, he won't get into the truck without a struggle, to say nothing about all the knocking about he'll have to endure along the way. I don't want to cause him any pain."

He mulled over her words for a moment. "People put their animals into trucks for journeys that last entire days."

"That's true," she conceded.

"The supply truck will be here tomorrow morning."

Sorrow washed into her voice. "We'll be gone by then."

For Um Qasem to announce her decision meant resigning herself to leaving Sabiliyat with no immediate prospect of returning. It was like being torn away against one's will and yet also with it at the same time. A bitter taste collected under her tongue. Good Omen planted his hooves before her and refused to budge. She understood full well that when he took the view that she should mount his back, it was because he felt a certain need for contact. Animals too have their finer shades of feeling. One had to give credit to the armies on both sides for having refrained from any shelling up to that point. Staying here would mean learning to live life under the bombs. "Let's go to Sayyid Rajab's shrine." She could cast a final look at the places that meant something to her. Good Omen broke into a brisk trot. As he turned into the lane he emitted a sharp snort. "What is it?" Her ears instantly made out the rumble of engines. She looked over her shoulder and saw a military Jeep making its way toward the Shatt. Following behind it was a small truck with a machine gun mounted on top and a soldier standing next to it. The rumble of the vehicles died away. "I won't have to get into any of their vehicles now."

Around half an hour later Second Lieutenant Sadeq came to find her.

"Lieutenant Abdel Kareem has had five men out looking for you."

She felt her knees buckling. "It's time to leave."

His reply took her aback.

"That's not what it's about." A broad grin appeared on his face. "My commander the Colonel has asked to see you."

She felt a need to express her misgivings. "I haven't done anything to necessitate that—"

He stopped her with the same line. "That's not what it's about."

She acquiesced to the inevitable. She turned to Good Omen. "You can go to the Daleeshiya orchard."

As they walked along side by side, Second Lieutenant Sadeq seized the opportunity to tell her, "I overheard part of a conversation that took place between my commander the Colonel and Lieutenant Abdel Kareem."

As she listened to him go on, she wondered to herself why he kept repeating the phrase "my commander" over and over.

When they'd been in touch with their command earlier on, Second Lieutenant Sadeq's report went, the latter had inquired about their urgent needs and Lieutenant Abdel Kareem had reassured them they were doing fine. His response had piqued their interest. All of the army units posted along the Shatt had had trouble meeting their needs for a whole two weeks, their platoon was the only one that, et cetera. When asked by his commander the Colonel how they'd managed to solve the problem of food, Lieutenant Abdel Kareem had replied it was all thanks to Um Qasem. That's why his commander the Colonel had asked to meet her. Um Qasem was unable to disguise her sense of anxiety. "May God shield us from harm."

The two of them were sitting together facing the Shatt. One of the men looked over forty and was wearing a uniform embroidered with red that had a number of gold badges on it.

This must be their colonel, she said to herself.

"Greetings," the Colonel began. "Our men here feel great appreciation toward you for the help you've given them."

"That's kind of them," she said with feeling.

"Lieutenant Abdel Kareem tells me you haven't finished burying your husband's remains because you're determined the two of you must stay together." He was silent for a moment. "You may go ahead and complete his burial rites." He added by way of qualification, "Should you choose to stay of your own accord."

Could she possibly be hearing what she thought she was? Her eyes darted to the face of Lieutenant Abdel Kareem, who seconded the other's words with a nod of assent. Her attention was consumed by the colonel's next question.

"Do you know how to read and write?"

She didn't ask, *"What's this got to do with anything?"* Instead she replied, "I learned to read the noble Qur'an and to write my name."

He said, "If you are to stay, you'll need to sign a declaration saying you're responsible for anything that happens to you."

"Oh Bu Qasem, you know what this war is like. You know it's still going strong and no one knows when it will be over. This is no time for declaring one's happiness, but I'll be honest with you, I'm so happy I could cry. I'll start scattering the soil over your remains this afternoon. There are more bricks at Mulla Hussein's house I can use. Good Omen and I will carry them together. I want you to have a handsome resting place."

- 14 -

IN ADDITION TO HER SICKLE SHE brought out a shovel. "Let's go, Good Omen." As she began walking along ahead of him she added, "We're going to Al-Halabi's to fetch some damask roses." Good Omen accelerated, overtook her, and blocked her path. A glow of pleasure spread inside her. She climbed onto his back. The most precious moments of her day were when she was sitting before Bu Qasem's grave talking with him and when she was standing before the Shatt, that living being, which rolled out evenly into infinity, relatively still from the outside but on the inside teeming with countless forms of life. She drew a deep breath into her chest and held it there for a moment. Ignoring a residual smell of gunpowder that still lingered in the air, she drank in the moistness, lush with the fragrance of wet loam. Her intuition told her that Good Omen was glad to be near the Shatt. She dismounted and watched him approach the embankment, steady himself with his hooves as he made his way down the muddy slope toward the water, and hold out his snout to drink his fill.

They continued on their course until they reached the spot where the thickets of damask rose were growing. The riot of freshly opened buds, she had been to this thicket before, why had she never breathed in the perfume of the roses so intensely?

Perhaps it was the sense of assurance she had that she was here to stay for an indefinite duration, and that she wasn't being threatened with expulsion at a specified time. She descended the slope and waded into the water that skirted the thicket from the direction of the Shatt. Her eyes fell on a number of vigorous-looking bushes whose branches were covered with blooming flowers. Using her sickle, she cleared away the longest branches and left the ones that had flowers on them. She then picked out four good-sized bushes and four smaller ones.

As she was crossing the Sayyid Rajab dam, a familiar hateful whistle reached her ears, followed by a loud explosion inside one of the houses. The blindness of a war caused by enmity. We won't give in to them, we'll go find where the shell landed and repair whatever we can. The sound of a cannon being fired somewhere nearby clapped through the air. Good Omen started with fright. One side declares its presence and the other responds in kind. The real war is taking place far away. She entered Al-Daleeshi's house. The bed around the Christ's-thorn tree was still moist. She planted two small saplings of damask rose and then watered them. The other pair of small saplings was meant for the house of Deaf Abboud. "Your roses are not just small saplings, Bu Qasem, they're full-grown bushes complete with flowers. I promised you that if God softened the hearts of the soldiers and they allowed us to stay, I'd make your home beautiful for you."

A week later Second Lieutenant Sadeq came to visit, accompanied by Private Jasem. The first expressed delight at the sight of the blooming roses, while the other pointed to the fronds of the Hilawi date palm.

"They're beginning to turn green."

She heaved out a sigh. "That won't last."

"Why not?" Private Jasem asked.

"Our rivers will dry up soon," she said. "Your dams are keeping the water from getting to them," she added.

"They're not our dams," Second Lieutenant Sadeq corrected her.

"What's the solution?" the other asked.

She didn't need long to come up with a reply. "The solution is in your hands." The men exchanged puzzled glances as Um Qasem pointed to her husband's grave and added, "Or maybe we can let Bu Qasem tell us what he thinks." Again the men exchanged glances.

One morning her ears picked up the rumble of heavy engines going past. She stepped out into the street and saw a number of army trucks hauling trailers mounted with oversized cannons, followed by a truck loaded with cannon shells of different sizes. They say it's a war of attrition, but she was still unable to fathom who was tiring out what.

She looked for opportunities to be alone with herself, she pondered ways of adjusting. The daytime hours didn't make her too anxious. So long as she could hear the shells coming, there was always the possibility of taking cover or flattening oneself on the ground to avoid the shrapnel, as Second Lieutenant Sadeq had advised her to do. The real problem was what to do with the hours of the night, when one lay sound asleep in one's bed. If a shell happened to land on the roof over her head...She didn't want to die away from her children. Her mind fell to work. There were no two ways about it, she had to take shelter in Sayyid Rajab's shrine.

She went into Deaf Abboud's carpentry workshop and

picked out a number of stakes of an equal length. With Good Omen's help, she carried them to the perimeter of Sayyid Rajab's shrine. She marked out a small area along the western wall of the building. This was where she'd build her shelter. She had no idea how Lieutenant Abdel Kareem got wind she was there, but suddenly he showed up accompanied by Second Lieutenant Sadeq and three soldiers.

"Nothing wrong I hope, Um Qasem?"

"I thought I'd put up a little lean-to," she explained.

He motioned to the soldiers, and they immediately threw themselves into work. Then he turned back to her and asked, "Who's the lean-to for?"

"For me," she replied, "so I can shelter here at night."

"What about your house?"

"My house won't protect me when the bombing gets bad."

"Who says it will get bad?"

"It will get bad," she replied with assurance.

"Was it Bu Qasem who told you?" he asked disbelievingly.

"No." She was silent for a moment and then she said, "But he came to visit me last night and he seemed unusually sad."

Lieutenant Abdel Kareem thought he'd humor her. "Why was he sad?" he asked with a show of interest.

"I don't know. But he went off in a rush taking the axe of our neighbor Deaf Abboud with him."

Lieutenant Abdel Kareem made no attempt to disguise his displeasure. "Here we go again," he muttered as if to himself. "I want to see you at the camp in an hour," he said to her curtly.

It would have breathed joy into her spirit to be approaching the Shatt had it not been for the gruffness Lieutenant Abdel Kareem had shown her. If only he knew the regard in which each and every one of her children held her. As she came up before his tent, she gave a light cough to let him know she'd arrived. She felt a little relieved to discover Second Lieutenant Sadeq was with him. He'd been planning to excuse himself, but his superior had asked him to stay. "Perhaps you understand Um Qasem better than I do." He turned around to face her.

"Should we be preparing ourselves to see the water break through our dams again?"

His voice was dark with displeasure.

"God knows best," she answered faintly.

"What are you not telling us?"

"Me?" she asked anxiously.

"What sort of coincidence is it that your husband appeared in your dreams, as you allege, right before these acts of sabotage took place that can only be perpetrated by..." He didn't finish his sentence.

Um Qasem's lips quivered but not a sound came out.

His voice grew steelier. "What exactly do you want?"

"Me?" she asked anxiously again.

"Why are you so dead set against the dams?"

"Me?"

"If it comes about that either dam—" he broke off, but then continued. "You'll be thrown out in a heartbeat."

Tears gathered in her eyes. "I can leave right this moment if you want."

Did some of the fire go out of Lieutenant Abdel Kareem? He turned to Second Lieutenant Sadeq.

"What are we to do with Um Qasem?"

"Why do you object to the dams?" Second Lieutenant Sadeq asked her in a sympathetic tone.

Her tongue was unlocked and the words rushed out. "Dams are a blessing when they hold back the water and a curse when they cut it off entirely."

"These dams were here when we arrived."

"They weren't here when we were evacuated."

"These dams were erected for military reasons."

Her voice grew gentler. "I don't understand your military reasons." She went on, "If you cut off the water from people and animals, they'll go look for it elsewhere. But trees will die where they stand."

He thought he'd play along. "What are you suggesting?"

"On my way over from Najaf, I passed by many dams that hadn't caused the trees to die. They'd laid down pipes along the riverbed and covered them with soil so that the water was able to get to the fields and people, and cars could also cross."

"This is a site of military operations."

Her voice grew even gentler. "There's no conflict between having pipes put under a dam and a place being a site of military…" She trailed off, perhaps her eyes grew a little misty.

Lieutenant Abdel Kareem asked her sympathetically, "You're concerned about the land getting watered."

"It's a sin to kill the fruit of the earth."

The upshot of their meeting, there were a few cement pipes lying around that would suit the purpose. To avoid giving the impression that he approved of the plan, Lieutenant Abdel Kareem said, "Tomorrow morning I'll be going up to the headquarters of our command with Private Jasem. We'll be leaving at dawn and we won't be back before sunset." He directed his closing words to his assisting officer.

"I don't want to know what takes place in my absence."

Second Lieutenant Sadeq smiled. "Orders received, Sir."

This accomplishment wasn't enough for Um Qasem. Before taking her leave, she put it to Lieutenant Abdel Kareem, "How nice it would be if we could buy some vegetable seeds."

"Some *what* seeds?"

"We could grow okra, cucumber, tomatoes, and the like."

"How do you mean?"

"Private Jasem knows about these kinds of things."

It didn't occur to her to wonder how the four rose bushes had grown so quickly. Their branches had shot up high, forming a bower that was bursting with open blooms. The Hilawi date palm looked greener and was putting out a lush yellow cluster of ripening dates. There was a straw mat spread over the ground under the trellis, lined with a few colored cushions made of wool. They were sitting across each other. She said to him with a significant air, knowing he was the only one who'd catch her meaning, "The children won't be home before nightfall." "Surely you don't plan to stay under this trellis until the night comes," Bu Qasem said disapprovingly. She eased into her question with a smile. "Are you annoyed?" She went on, "I've had to start building another lean-to at Sayyid Rajab's shrine for fear that..." She let her sentence dangle. She began again. "When the bombing gets bad, it doesn't affect you."

She was surprised to hear him ask, "Did you really mean what you said about growing vegetables?" She thought it best to reassure him. "Our soldiers won't think twice about lending a hand." She had the impression he was deep in thought. "Lieutenant Abdel Kareem, Second Lieutenant Sadeq, the cement pipes." "I don't follow," she said to him chidingly. "All this labor of yours…" He broke off. "What is it that bothers you?" she asked him. "It's a lot of work." "I'm not alone." He sprung to his feet. "Are you angry with me?" she asked him beseechingly. She was stunned by his response. "I'm angry *for* you." There was something about the way he said this that she couldn't understand. "What do you mean?" "You're wearing yourself out." She laughed. He stretched out his hand. "Come with me." She put her hand in his. All of a sudden he vanished from before her. "Where are you?" There was no one there to hear. She was sitting upright in the middle of her bed. That tingling in her palm, the unshakeable sense of having just felt the touch of his hand. It was a little before dawn, the same time as all her other dreams.

After Lieutenant Abdel Kareem had departed with Private Jasem, Second Lieutenant Sadeq kept six soldiers posted by the cannons opposite the Shatt al-Arab and divided the rest into three groups. To the first he assigned the task of hauling ten large cement pipes from the dumping ground, with instructions to deposit five of these by the dam on Sayyid Rajab River and the other five at the dam on Chouma. The second group had the task of clearing a passage through the soil on the Sayyid Rajab dam, while the third had the same task for the dam on Chouma River. They started digging around six in the morning. The water on the Shatt al-Arab was at a complete ebb at that time. They finished a little before nine just as the tide was beginning to rise in the Shatt. They laid down the cement pipes, five along each river bed, and then put everything back the way it was. As the tide rose, the water began rushing toward the interior with startling force.

15

"IF YOU TRIED PLOUGHING THIS ORCHARD all on your own, it would take you six months to finish."

"God bless your helping hands."

Working together under Private Jasem's directions, ten soldiers set about shoveling through the soil of Um Al-Barhee orchard. Then they smoothed the ground over and traced out a grid of parallel rectangles. It took them seven days to finish that work.

"What would you like to plant first?" Private Jasem asked her.

A sense of excitement overcame her. "Everything!"

A week later the green shoots of okra, sunflowers, and corn began to break through the top of the soil. Private Jasem didn't have to put up a scarecrow in the middle of the newly planted field to ward off any birds that might come poaching as they had not yet returned to nest.

"Some types of pulses can be left to their own devices if we plant the seeds at a particular level right beside the creeks where the tide can reach them twice a day. We might as well plant some cowpeas, green beans, and broad beans."

"The way the water ebbs and rises here is different from what you see in Al-Faw."

Um Qasem listened carefully as Private Jasem went on.

"Over there our rivers flush out all their water during the ebb down to the last drop, so you can see right down to their red spongy bed. It's because the fields slope toward the Shatt and because they're close to the Gulf."

"I gather from what you say that your water is briny and no good for drinking."

"It seems briny to people who aren't used to it." He went on, "But our land is fertile, you plant a banana seedling near the river and within six months it's shot up so high it's outdoing the oldest mulberry trees. And don't get me started on its fruit—the citrons, the lemons, oranges, tangerines, apricots, grapes!"

She listened on as he began enthusiastically describing the vessels they'd use for extracting date syrup.

"We'd fill up hundreds of cans with date syrup after the harvest season was over."

There was little doubt left in her mind, Jasem's love for the land rivaled hers.

The days rolling by, bringing a sense of accomplishment in their wake. The rose seedlings kept putting out flower after flower, while the various pulses planted in Um Al-Barhee orchard were streaking it with different shades of green. The bombardment carried on at its usual pace. It would stop during the day, and it would seem as if some truce must have been unexpectedly called, only for it to gather force again at night provoking a sense of anxiety and dread that were her mind's way of saying: death is standing at the doorstep. Or again it would grow fierce in the daytime hours, doubling

154

down on its mysterious targets out there, and then it would ease up at night so that you'd start wishing you could let yourself sink into a deep peaceful sleep, except you couldn't because then you might fail to catch the sound of a shell whistling toward you.

Adjusting to the circumstances, trying to learn to live with them. Um Qasem would spend the first hour of the morning sitting alone with Bu Qasem and talking things over with him. Then she'd go around the houses that had recently been hit to inspect the damage, those eyesores couldn't be allowed to stay like that. After obtaining permission from Lieutenant Abdel Kareem, Private Jasem volunteered to accompany her on these inspection missions and help her carry out her repair work. She divided her late mornings and evenings between Um Al-Barhee orchard and her little shelter on the western wall of Sayyid Rajab's shrine, which stood only a few meters from the main entrance to the orchard.

"Where did you get these rose seedlings?" Private Jasem asked her one day.

Without asking why he wanted to know, she turned to Good Omen and directed him to show the way the thicket.

Private Jasem gaped in disbelief. "You're telling a donkey to—"

"Quick or you might lose him," she prompted.

He saw Good Omen making off at a brisk trot. He swiftly set off after him. An hour later he returned with four flowering shoots of damask rose hitched to Good Omen's back. Her heart skipped with pleasure.

"Where will you plant them?"

"Here." He pointed to the area right in front of the shelter.

She couldn't stop the tears from welling up in her eyes. It wasn't right that he should see her agitation, she turned her face away. "That's too much," she murmured to herself.

As the summer heat intensified and the dates began to ripen in July, it became a regular source of refreshment to sit inside the shelter in the late morning. Seizing the opportunity as he sat by Um Qasem's side, Private Jasem said, "I'm finding it a little difficult calling you 'Um Qasem.'"

She frowned at him. "What's difficult about it?"

He didn't respond to her question directly. "I feel I'd like to say *Mother*."

Her eyes sparkled with pleasure. "I have three sons, you're now my fourth."

Once he told her his story. The only thing he could remember from his early years was the mud house they used to live in and his mother's chickens. He didn't have any brothers or sisters, his mother had died before he was three, and his father had followed in her footsteps only a few months later. He grew to awareness living under his uncle's roof. His voice softened with feeling.

"As good or bad luck would have it, my uncle had no offspring of his own. My aunt was a kindhearted woman and she made sure I had everything I needed. We had two male dogs that used to spend most of their time play-fighting, and my aunt would wade in like a third party to the dispute."

The last description made Um Qasem laugh. "Where are they now?"

Perhaps the question took him by surprise, or perhaps he didn't catch her meaning. She added by way of clarification, "I mean, do you know how your family is doing?"

He was away on military service when the evacuation orders were issued.

"As soon as the war is over they'll return home," she said soothingly. His reply took her aback.

"What home? Everyone who follows the news knows that Al-Faw in particular has been shelled thousands of times in the three years since the war started." He drew a sharp breath. "Not a single stone has been left standing. Apparently they've taken the decision to occupy it."

She understood that the reference was to the other side. "First they destroy it and then they occupy it," she said with vexation. He turned around to make sure no one was overhearing. "We too destroyed a number of their cities on the frontier."

If it was up to her she'd have nothing to do with talk of war. She hated war to begin with.

Autumn was heralding the approach of winter when out of the blue Private Jasem floated the idea they should find a way to put the date surplus to use.

"Let's set up a press for extracting the syrup." His imagination was racing ahead as he spoke. "The syrup of Barhee dates is as sweet as honey, in fact it leaves honey in the dust when it comes to taste and aroma."

As the mastermind of the idea, he set about putting it into action. The construction of a basin raised about a meter off the ground, the working of incisions all along the bottom of the basin, connecting these to narrow ducts that fed into a receptacle of appropriate size.

"After we fill the basin with dates, we press them as hard

157

as we can and then we give them a chance to drain out their juices."

Soon the press was ready to receive its first batch of dates.

One night the bombardment was heavier than usual. One shell landed on the part of the camp where Private Jasem had his tent. The soldier who was sleeping right next to him was killed instantaneously, while Private Jasem felt a strange kind of numbness creeping up his left arm. The shock of those first moments, the bewilderment, the mind frozen, the shredded limbs of his comrade strewn all around him—he was unable to take in what had happened. It was Second Lieutenant Sadeq who noticed and tried to stanch the blood pouring out of his wrist. Private Jasem was stunned to see the white of his wrist bone sticking out.

"I've lost my hand." His consciousness was starting to give, he asked in a flickering voice, "Where is she?"

The military ambulance showed up around noon. The arrangements began for transporting the body parts of the soldier who had been killed and the one who had been injured. In his right hand he clutched a small piece of folded cloth containing the shattered remains of his left hand. Before climbing into the vehicle, Private Jasem said to Second Lieutenant Sadeq, "Will you save a spot for me in the graveyard?"

He placed the cloth with the shattered bone in his hands. The rest of the soldiers felt a sense of bereavement. A thick cloud of gloom hung over them that entire day.

"There's no one else I can share my trouble with but you,

Bu Qasem. It's a terrible thing for a young soldier like that to be killed while lying in his bed. I don't think you'll say he died without realizing, or he felt no pain as death took him. I don't know. I didn't know that young boy well. I only found out his name after he was killed. He was called Adnan and he came from Samarra. They collected his remains in a plastic bag. You may not believe me, but what really got to me was Private Jasem's hand being torn off and his leaving us to go I know not where. I told you he asked me if he could call me 'Mother,' and you know how much happiness this fourth son of mine gave me. You can't put a price on it, that pure feeling of maternal tenderness that wells up in you just watching him come and go.

"I didn't go to see him off, I wasn't sure I'd be able to bear it. I went to the funeral in which they buried some of Private Adnan's effects and my son Jasem's hand. Should I be a little more cheerful, Bu Qasem? Jasem is still alive after all. Or should I feel sad because he lost his hand? Should I feel happy because he got the chance to leave the war zone, or should I feel sad because I can no longer see him before me every day? It gave me a secret rush to hear him call me 'Mother.' It was he who independently took the decision to become my son. Jasem lost a hand, but I lost the whole of him. It seems to me we only find out the value things have for us after they're gone."

After the dark had fallen, Second Lieutenant Sadeq came around accompanied by Private Mazen. He handed her a paper bag containing a few pieces of army bread.

"Lieutenant Abdel Kareem was wondering where you are. He sent us over to bring you some of the bread you like."

"We looked for you at the shelter but you weren't there,"

the other chipped in.

"Will you be spending the night here?"

She wasn't quite sure why she motioned vaguely toward the grave. "I don't know what Bu Qasem will decide." She had the sense they were struggling hard not to betray the sorrow they felt over the events of the previous day, but the bitterness lining their voices gave it away.

Before they took their leave, Private Mazen spoke up. "I'll be at the orchard of Um Al-Barhee tomorrow morning." She nodded in acknowledgment.

"You have three living sons, and you feel all this distress about a fourth that wasn't even the fruit of your own womb." She tried to mollify him, her voice grew tender. "I find it hard to believe this is the reason you're so upset." "I'm upset because of how sad you're feeling." "We don't get to decide how happy or sad we feel," she replied. "If you say so," he relented. They were sitting across from each other on a straw mat in front of the shelter at Sayyid Rajab's shrine. His attention drifted to the rose shrubs. "They're the same type as the ones planted by my graveside," he observed. "It was my fourth son who came up with the idea," she was quick to point out. "Well now, if he planted it…" he trailed off for a moment and then continued confidently, "He'll come back to make sure it's being looked after." She was overcome by surprise. "What makes you so sure?" "The love he has for you." "You're talking nonsense," she chided him. But he went on, "Also because of the love you have for him." "You're really exaggerating things." His reply left her speechless: "There's no room for exaggeration when it comes to the purest love."

A strong gust of wind suddenly blew in, ruffling the sheet

of canvas that was draped over the shelter. She looked up to see what was happening and when she looked back he was no longer there. "Bu Qasem!" she cried out in terror. The shelter faded into nothing. She sat bolt upright in her bed. The sound of Good Omen's snorts reached her from the other side of the half-closed door. It had to be dawn or a little after that. She got out of bed. Good Omen greeted her with enthusiasm. He put out his head for her, and she patted it affectionately.

She was standing beside the date press. "We shouldn't let Private Jasem down."

Private Mazen looked at her in puzzlement.

"Let's fill the basin with dates," she proposed.

A wan smile crossed his face. "We'll need someone to help us cut down the dates, round them up and clean them. And then..." he broke off. His voice rang with melancholy when he resumed, "If Jasem was here..."

She interrupted him with conviction. "He'll be here."

A look of astonishment swept over his features. "Did he tell you that?"

"No."

His astonishment did not abate. "Then how do you know?"

She didn't have to think long. "Bu Qasem told me." She added, "The dead don't lie." She heard him muttering to himself in confusion, "I don't know what to say."

"You have no reasons to be doubtful."

He mulled these words over. Then a question occurred to him. "When will he be back?"

"He won't be long," she said. "Bu Qasem didn't specify

161

a day," she added.

Private Mazen turned things over in his mind. "We'll need to consult Second Lieutenant Sadeq. We'll need several hands on deck if we're to operate the date press." With encouragement from Second Lieutenant Sadeq, four soldiers with farming experience who knew how to pick, clean, and stack dates volunteered to help.

Late one morning while they were at work Lieutenant Abdel Kareem asked to see her. "I want this conversation to stay between us."

She did her best to hide her sense of apprehension. "Your secret is safe with me," she promised.

"What I want to talk about relates to you," he began carefully.

"Have you taken the decision to expel me?"

"That's not what it's about."

She sighed out helplessly. "I wish you'd speak openly," she said.

"You know how much everyone respects you, Um Qasem."

She couldn't find anything to say in reply.

"Apart from the fact that everyone respects you, they take everything you say very seriously."

If only she could tell him she wasn't following.

He went on, "Our soldiers are simple folk with a strong religious feeling."

If only she could ask what he was getting at.

"We don't want them to start putting anyone on a pedestal and thinking they're some kind of saint."

She could no longer contain herself. "I don't understand

what you're saying," she broke out.

"There are soldiers going around saying Um Qasem can foresee the future."

She gave a shudder. "God have mercy on us." Immediately she asked, "Are you asking me to leave?"

His response took her aback. "I want you to stay, on condition that we don't let our fancy run away with us."

She felt her sense of composure returning. "What do you mean?"

"You haven't seen Private Jasem since he was injured, correct?"

"Correct."

"So he didn't personally convey to you this fanciful intention of his to return."

"I'm finding it hard to follow the things you're saying."

"Let me ask you, do you know where they took Private Jasem?"

"I have no idea."

"And yet you've put a rumor about that he'll be coming back soon."

"I didn't—" She was silent for a moment. "It was Bu Qasem who—" She was suddenly aware of how feeble her claim sounded. "I'll do as you order," she said meekly.

Lieutenant Abdel Kareem's tone softened. "Private Jasem is at the Teaching Hospital in Baghdad. Under the present circumstances it's impossible for anyone to make contact with him."

She drew a deep breath conveying tentative relief.

"What happens if he doesn't come back within the next month?"

She mustered her resolve. "If what Bu Qasem said was

false, I'll pack my things and go back to Najaf."

He shook his head mournfully. "Perhaps you don't know…" he trailed off. He continued, "Soldiers who suffer major injuries are automatically relieved of military duty."

16

WHY THIS CLOUD OVER HER SPIRIT, why did things have to be casting clouds? When she now reflected on her relationship to the place, to the soldiers in general, to Lieutenant Abdel Kareem in particular, she couldn't see anything she had done wrong, anything to make her doubt or accuse herself. If she'd simply been ordered to leave and that's that, she would have been able to cope with that. It hurt her more that they should make her ability to stay depend on things that lay outside her control. When she'd casually exchanged a few words with one of the soldiers, when she'd told him Private Jasem would be coming back, it had never crossed her mind the rumor would start that she could tell the future. That's something only God could know. As far as she was concerned, all it came down to was a specific message Bu Qasem had communicated to her. He'd looked at the rose bushes and predicted the person who'd planted them would come back.

She remembered something her son Saleh had teasingly said to her one day when she was still living with them in Najaf. "The truth is, you rustle up my father in your sleep so he can tell you what you want to hear." She remembers protesting, "Stuff and nonsense. Your father has never visited me for my pleasure." She remembers how her other son Hameed had countered his brother. "No one can willfully contrive to have the dreams they'd like to have." Saleh's voice floats back to her. "If anyone can it's my mother." Her eldest son Qasem had stepped in and put an end to the debate. "Even while my father was alive the two of them were two hearts beating as one."

Her sons' voices made her mind travel back. The happy cries of her grandsons and granddaughters drifted up to her. She felt a throb of longing. Being looked after, having a sense of standing. Maybe she'd been too hasty taking the decisions that had brought her where she was. The sadness nested inside her. "What do you think, Good Omen?" He bowed his head. "What if we were to make our way back to Najaf?" She leaned in toward him. He didn't make his familiar snort. She continued, "We'll disappear without anyone knowing. They'll get up in the morning and we'll be gone." When Private Mazen asked her, "How many dates should we put inside the basin of the syrup press?" she replied languidly, "I don't know." He gave her a look of disappointment. "It's up to you how you handle your own affairs," she added with a toss of her hand. She had taken her leave early and made her way home.

"Where's the mistake, Bu Qasem, can you tell me? Is it me, is it you, or is it the others? People sometimes say, 'So-and-so has pure intentions.' I know my intentions are pure, I never harbored evil intentions against anyone or had thoughts I wanted to harm anyone, all I wanted was for you and me to be here together. Despite all the love and attention our sons showered on me, the yearning to be home made me weather the hardship of the journey, the dangers lurking everywhere, the threat of being chased away at a moment's notice. And when I was finally given a chance to stay with everyone's consent, this thing happens which I don't need to tell you about because you had a hand in it too."

The sun had not yet set that day when the shelling began hard. This time she didn't seek refuge in her shelter at Sayyid Rajab's shrine. It moved her to pity to see the state Good Omen was in. He was shaking all over from fear. "If it's our fate to die today, then we will die no matter whether we stay at home or go to the shelter." She brought him a saucer with soaked bean seeds and date kernels. The sour fragrance of the sumptuous dish made him forget his fear and he fell upon it with relish. An hour later the shelling stopped.

"You're a woman who's too sensitive for her own good." "During our whole life together you never said such things to me," she protested. They were lying side by side on their bed. He rolled his head toward her and said, "Honesty is one of the parts of love." She reached out and stroked his face. "You're my dear love." He brought her hand to his lips and kissed it. "You shouldn't forget how much you went through to get to Sabiliyat." There was a tone of bereavement in the way he uttered the last word. "You speak about Sabiliyat as if you weren't living in it," she replied reproachfully. "Maybe it's because of the thoughts filling your mind as you get ready to leave." "It's not up to me whether I stay or go."

He lifted his head a little and gazed deeply into her eyes. "We shouldn't let our relations with our men be governed by the logic of provocation." A sense of astonishment came over her. "What provocation?" "Remember the promise you made, if Private Jasem isn't back within a month…" He was silent for a few moments. "The bonds we share with them require us to treat them with understanding." She felt his hand tenderly pressing on hers. "There was a time when you only had three sons." She caught his drift and hastened to declare, "Now I have four." She was stunned to hear him say, "You're wrong." She didn't try to disguise the injury she felt. "Does my having a fourth son displease you?" He smiled. "Your sons number over forty." She laughed. "You're overstating things." "The dead don't overstate." "I know you mean well." She reached over with her arm to pull him close but she felt her hand sinking into the void.

Her senses rallied. Alone in the darkness of the room. Her ears caught the sound of something whistling overhead followed by a thundering explosion in the dumping ground behind her house. She huddled in her bed. There they were again resuming their bombardment. The shredded limbs of a young soldier, Jasem's left hand. "When will this war end, Bu Qasem?" Loud blasts followed in close succession, some coming from nearby and others from farther away. A sense of conviction suddenly took hold of her. This war they'd got started will keep going for years. Even though she knew Bu Qasem backed the idea of her staying, even though she was wrung out by the longing to be there and nowhere else, the thought crystallized within her: things were no longer the same. War had harsh rules of its own. Lieutenant Abdel Kareem had spoken the final word as the one in command, the deadline was fixed. She searched her thoughts. There was no room for her to simply revise her position by offering an apology. She couldn't simply present herself to him and say, "I'm sorry, I won't repeat what I said about…" It wasn't about having made some mistake that carried a finite set of repercussions. It was the war with its infinite repercussions.

Before the first lights of dawn had broken, the exchange of fire began to let up until it finally came to a stop. "Let's go, Good Omen." He trotted out of the door ahead of her and then stopped short expectantly. She understood his request. She climbed onto his back. "Let's go to Private Jasem's grave." A wry smile appeared on her face. "Jasem isn't dead." She added, "We'll read the opening verse of the Qur'an for his hand."

Second Lieutenant Sadeq saw her standing by the grave-stone and came up to her.

"I don't want to say you went too far on the issue of Private Jasem coming back."

She looked at him fixedly hoping she might catch his drift.

"None of the soldiers who were given the opportunity to be relieved of service ever came back."

Silently she wondered what he was trying to tell her.

"Between you and me," he confided, "there have been numerous cases of soldiers posted on the front who shot them-selves in the foot so as to incur a handicap that would allow them to be relieved of service."

"I don't follow."

"Private Jasem won't be coming back," he replied tersely. "However much we might wish it," he added.

"God be our helper," she replied as if to herself.

The days were racing by in a countdown to the deadline she'd set herself with Lieutenant Abdel Kareem. Strange new emotions began to crowd upon her. Grief mixed with a sense of helplessness, a leaden kind of gloom she'd never experienced before, an inability to sleep that was beyond her powers of endurance. "What do you advise me to do, Bu Qasem?" Yet Bu Qasem had stopped visiting her dreams every other night as he used to. Sleep came to her fitfully only a few hours at a time. When she finally managed to drop off after long hours lying awake, she sank into a dumb dreamless stupor. There was nothing holding her there, nothing forcing her to leave straight away. The deadline had almost run its course. One question she couldn't entirely banish from her mind. What would happen to the houses that were hit by shells and needed to have their walls repaired, and also to the scrap metal from the shells that would need to be collected and taken to the dump?

Late one morning Private Mazen showed up at her doorstep.

"You haven't been looking in on Um Al-Barhee orchard," he said in a tone of reproachful surprise. "It's been three weeks since—"

"I'll follow you there shortly," she stopped him. She ran her eyes over the orchard without enthusiasm.

"Is something wrong, Um Qasem?" Private Mazen asked her with affectionate concern.

"It looks like I'll be heading back to Najaf soon."

He didn't try to disguise the pang of sorrow he felt. "It never entered our thoughts that you were considering leaving."

A melancholy smile lit her face. "I've missed my children and grandchildren." She saw Lieutenant Abdel Kareem before her again, what he'd said about the soldiers and about rumors that excite speculation. "I don't want anyone else to know about my intention to travel to Najaf," she appealed to him. "I'll let them know myself when the time is right," she added.

"You have my word," he assured her.

In the final week she felt an urge to go through all the familiar places and have a look around them. She would let her eyes feast on little details as if she were trying to store up the images in her memory. There was the house of Mahmoud Abbas, it gave her heart to see the Bambawi Christ's-thorn tree bursting with dark green leaves again. Second Lieutenant Sadeq would be able to look after the rose seedlings that were growing taller by the day. The house of Jawad Al-Daleeshi, the Christ's-thorn tree with the fleshy fruit. She had restored it to its original vitality, its branches dotted all over with green new buds. The house of Deaf Abboud, the plum tree and the damask rose bushes.

On the morning of the day before her last, she decided to take Good Omen with her on a slow promenade down the coast of the Shatt al-Arab. This sheet of water rolling into the horizon, its surface rippling ceaselessly, life thrashing in the deep. She drew a long breath that filled her lungs. There was a light stench of fish in the moist air. It made her smart to picture a cannon going off at any moment from one direction or the other, the shelling intensifying overhead across the waters of the Shatt. If only she could understand why they were so determined to keep going with this pointless war. She remembered what her son Saleh had said one day six months after the war had broken out. During their time in Najaf the whole family would regularly convene inside her shack. "I don't understand what was the point of our having gone to war with them." Her eldest son Qasem fixed him with a disapproving glare. "Be careful you don't go about saying such things in the open." Saleh smiled. "I'm in my own home." "Even the walls have ears," Qasem shot back. They had started this war three years ago in the autumn. It was autumn now. What had either side gotten out of...?

On her way back from her promenade as she was walking past the area where the army tents stood, she caught sight of Lieutenant Abdel Kareem stepping out of his tent and motioning to her. Her heart missed a beat. It flashed through her mind that he'd want to use the opportunity to remind her when the deadline ran out. She dismounted from Good Omen's back while he strode toward her. "Good day to you." There was a friendly smile playing in his eyes. Should she feel surprised at his manner or should she take things as they came? "You're not obliged to stick to your promise," he said to her. The word "obliged" was painful taken on its own, what was the use of suggesting to someone that they could be exempted from doing what they had to do when the sun next rose. The expression of sympathy is sometimes an insult even if one means well.

"Thank you," she said. Then she went on, "But I've made up my mind." The smile vanished from his face. She had the sense he was about to say something, but she turned around and walked away trying to hide the tears in her eyes.

The pain turning you inside out like an iron clamp pressing into your flesh. "I don't know how you think, Bu Qasem. If you really want me to be honest with you, even though I don't know how you think, I'll tell you, I was going about my life among the soldiers, alongside them, as if I was one of them, the shells coming and going in their usual way. Then when I lost my fourth son Jasem, getting fired up with the hope he'd be back... You're the one who said he'd be back." She was sitting in a crouch opposite the grave. "I hope you can understand me. Please accept my honesty even if you find it annoying."

She was silent for a moment. "On the outskirts of Nasiriya on our way over, when your sons gathered together around your grave in that wondrous way and the idea was aired to dig up your remains, I appealed to a last will and testament you hadn't made and I told our sons, 'He wanted to be buried where he was born.' The truth was that I was the one who wanted that. Our sons stood there looking stunned, not knowing what to do. It's not in their character to disobey us when we ask them to do something. You know everything that happened next so I don't need to tell you. What you don't know is—" she broke off and heaved out a pained sigh. "I won't dig up your grave a second time. I won't take you with me on my journey back." Her mind drifted for a moment. "Since the time you declared to me that Private Jasem would be coming back you haven't visited me in my sleep. I don't want to criticize you, but I'll tell you openly, my heart tells me this grave is the best place for you. Don't get angry with me or reproach me. If you were to ask me what things have been like for me, after you left me, I ceased to have a use in the world. I don't want to rattle on... You know my decision."

Good Omen poked his head through the door of the pen making a sound like a sneeze. "What is it?" Her ears picked up the rumble of an engine somewhere outside. Some vehicle was making its way toward the army camp, perhaps it was their supply truck. She reflected for a moment. If she was to depart the next morning, she ought to see Private Mazen or Second Lieutenant Sadeq and ask one of them to keep up with a few minor chores. She would be sad to leave her little shelter by Sayyid Rajab's shrine, but this was how things were. She should also show them where to find the containers with the pickled vegetables in Deaf Abboud's house, for them to enjoy. Beyond that, she had to start getting ready, though she didn't need to do much. She still had a bit of money left that she could use to get by on the journey back.

Good Omen poked his head through the door for a second time. "What is it?" A few seconds passed before she began to hear a hum of voices approaching. If Second Lieutenant Sadeq was with them she could take the opportunity to convey her requests to him. She glanced at the door, it was half-open as usual. Moments passed, the hum of voices broke off. Someone was knocking on the door.

"It's open," she called out.

Second Lieutenant Sadeq put his head through the door.

"How are you, Um Qasem?"

He didn't give her a chance to return his greeting, he immediately drew back and she heard him telling someone, "Wait here." He stepped inside and closed the door behind him. It was clear he didn't want the person standing outside to overhear what he had to say.

"Lieutenant Abdel Kareem has asked me to…"

It was something about a misunderstanding and about rushing to decisions, the other party shouldn't judge too harshly… he would therefore like to express his regret for having been so rough with Um Qasem. She should know that when he saw her a few hours ago, he tried to explain certain circumstances to her…She interrupted him pleading,

"Speak to me in words I can understand."

He smiled apologetically and went on.

"Lieutenant Abdel Kareem wasn't comfortable with the things he'd said even though no one thought it likely that

Private Jasem would come back."

"Just don't rub salt into wounds," she felt like imploring him.

He continued, "Yesterday evening he received a message from our command asking him whether he had any objections against the possibility of Private Jasem returning to active duty in line with the express desire of the latter."

Her breathing almost stopped as she took in the meaning of Second Lieutenant Sadeq's words.

"If only you could have seen how happy Lieutenant Abdel Kareem was. He gave his approval instantly. After he had finished his exchange, he turned to me and said, 'Um Qasem was right.'"

Gathering resolve she asked, "Is he…?" She trailed off as her voice grew hoarse with emotion.

"He arrived with the supply truck. Just a moment…"

Second Lieutenant Sadeq went to the door and pushed it open. Private Jasem stepped inside.

Her knees buckled beneath her, and her body slumped to the ground. Private Jasem rushed over and caught her in his right arm.

"Steady, Mother."

It was his voice just as she remembered it. She noticed he was using only his right arm. His left hand was tucked inside one of the pockets of his vest just next to where she could see a small leather pouch fixed to his belt. She reached out and felt for the stub of his arm inside his pocket.

"Does it hurt?" she asked.

He gave a quick laugh and drawing his arm out of his pocket he motioned toward the spot where it had been amputated.

"I feel pain in my fingers."

"But your fingers are no longer there," she observed with somber surprise.

"Every now and then I get a feeling of pain or fatigue in my fingers. My right hand goes out and tries to wrap itself around my left-hand fingers. I consulted the doctor at the Teaching Hospital and he pointed to my head and said, 'This is where your pain comes from. In a few months' time your mind will finally take things in and realize your hand is no longer there.'"

Just that moment there was no room for feeling sad.

"I hope you feel better soon," she murmured.

Using his right hand, he reached over into his small pouch and pulled out a shiny metal hook with a leather strap coming out the other end.

"This is what makes up for my missing hand now."

He fumbled for a few moments while he fitted the hook onto the stub of his arm. Then he asked, "How are things with our syrup press?"

She didn't need to think long.

"We were waiting for you to come back." She sprung to her feet. "Now we can get back to work."